DOUBLE TROUBLE
mansion mystery

Michael J. Pellowski

digital cover illustration by Michael Petty
inside illustrations by Mel Crawford

To Morgan (Baron Bolligrew).
Your fame still grows.

First printing by Willowisp Press 1998.

Published by PAGES Publishing Group
801 94th Avenue North, St. Petersburg, Florida 33702

Printed in the United States of America

Willowisp Press ®

2 4 6 8 10 9 7 5 3 1

ISBN 0-87406-892-4

CHAPTER **One**

How? How do you say good-bye to someone who has been a trusted and true friend your entire life? What words do you use? When I learned last summer that my best friend's dad was being transferred to another state and that she was moving before the start of school, I was speechless. I couldn't imagine starting fifth grade without my best friend Jamie Collins at my side.

Before she left, I wanted to tell Jamie how special our friendship was to me. I wanted to thank her for special things like never squealing on us whenever my identical twin sister Randi and I pulled the "old switcheroo" and traded identities to trick everyone from the school soccer coach to the class bully. I also wanted to thank her for never confusing Sandi and Randi Daniels. She could always tell us apart, even when I wasn't wearing my glasses. (I'm slightly near-sighted. Randi isn't.) I wanted Jamie to know how important it was to me when she remembered little things like who my favorite romance writer was or who Randi's favorite pro soccer player was. I wanted to say those things and lots more. But what I wanted to say I couldn't say—and didn't say.

I think it's totally weird that a person like me who loves to read and write stories couldn't find the right words to say good-bye to someone whom my twin sister and I had shared most of our secrets with over the years. Since I couldn't think of a way to say good-bye to my best friend, I didn't. When Jamie left town, instead of saying good-bye, I made a promise. I promised to phone her once a week, every week, forever. I intended to be close friends with Jamie despite the huge distance between us. We both swore we'd always stay in touch.

Sandi Daniels always keeps her word.

I called Jamie every week until Dad complained that our phone bill was out of this world. After my parents limited my long distance calls to one a month, I started writing letters to Jamie instead. Normally I did my letter writing at home on Friday nights while my sister Randi watched sports on TV with my dad and Trouble. Trouble was our nickname for our three-year-old brother, Teddy. Trouble was attracted to Teddy like bears to honey.

Last Friday night when I sat down to write Jamie a long letter about the new book of true ghost stories I was reading, Trouble lived up to his nickname. I heard a loud crash. Then Trouble started screaming.

"Caw nine won won!" he yelled. "Fish emergenshee! Fish emergenshee!"

I jumped up from my desk chair and ran out into the hall. I couldn't believe my eyes! Teddy had accidentally smashed our fish tank with the miniature baseball bat Dad had bought him. All of the water had gushed out of the tank and fish were flopping around everywhere on the soggy carpet.

"I hitta homer, Sanee!" Teddy said. "It wuzza accident."

My parents, my sister, and I spent the rest of Friday night cleaning up the mess. During the weekend we had to buy a new fish tank and then set it up. I never did get around to writing Jamie my weekly letter. In order to live up to my pledge, I decided to dash off a quick note to Jamie at school on Monday. I would drop the letter off at the post office when Randi and I walked home. It was a good plan, but it had one flaw: writing a letter at school wouldn't be easy.

"What are you doing?" Randi whispered as she leaned across the aisle toward me. Randi and I were both in Miss Morgan's fifth-grade class. She was a hard teacher, but she was fair and fun. We liked her a lot.

Plus, Miss Morgan was more than just our teacher. She was also a friend of our parents. Miss Morgan and our mom belonged to the local historical society. They were both interested in our town's history. In fact, Miss Morgan's ancestors were some of our town's founding fathers.

I leaned over and whispered back to my sister, "I'm going to write a letter to Jamie." She nodded as I sneaked a piece of purple writing paper out of my folder. Purple and pink were my two favorite colors.

"You're going to get in trouble," Randi said softly. "We're supposed to be working on our essays about the American Revolution." Our class was studying America's War of Independence and its effect on the town where we lived. Our town was very old. It was settled way before the American Revolution. "Miss Morgan gave us free time to do classwork, not for you to write Jamie notes about which boys got cuter since she moved away," Randi said, teasing.

I pushed my glasses up the bridge of my nose until they were snug against my face and then shot my sister a mean look.

"Which one of us gets *As* in social studies and which one of us gets *Bs*?" I whispered back. Randi and I were identical twins, but we were not identical in a lot of ways. I was the studious twin and Randi was the athletic twin. I was more emotional and sentimental and Randi was outspoken and hot-tempered. My comment about our grades caused Randi's famous temper to flare up. She gritted her teeth and gave me a nasty look before getting back to work on her essay. Our essays were due at the end of the week. I'd already done extra work on mine, so writing a letter to Jamie wouldn't put me behind.

I started off my letter with the usual I'm-fine-how-goes-it-with-you? stuff. Then I quickly turned my attention to telling Jamie about the book of true ghost stories I'd just finished. Because I believed in ghosts, I found the stories fascinating. One story about the ghost of a little girl who haunted a public library gave me chills whenever I thought about it. I was so busy writing about the story of the little girl's ghost that I didn't hear Miss Morgan approaching my desk. It wasn't until my classmates started snickering that I realized I was busted but good. I looked up. Miss Morgan was staring down at me.

"Do you mind if I read your essay to the class?"

Miss Morgan asked me. Without waiting for a reply, she snatched the piece of purple writing paper off my desk. I sighed loudly and fidgeted in my seat as Miss Morgan's eyes scanned the words on the page. I sneaked a peek at my twin. Randi silently mouthed the words, "I told you so."

"Now this is an interesting essay on the American Revolution," Miss Morgan announced to my classmates. She waved my note in the air and then began to read it. "Sandi writes, *'True Ghost Stories for the Faint of Heart* is the best book on ghosts I have ever read. The scary tale of little Lucy Lovecraft, the lost ghost of the library, was so frightening that I had to sleep with the lights on the night I read it.'"

Everyone in the class burst into laughter. I sunk down low in my seat.

"I always knew Sandi was a big chicken," said Bobbi Joy Boikin, the class pain-in-the-neck. Bobbi flapped her arms and made chicken noises. The class, including my sister Randi, laughed even louder.

Miss Morgan continued, "'The story sent shivers

down my spine and gave me goose bumps. If I hadn't already believed in ghosts, I sure would now.'"

"HARR! HARR!" howled Bobbi Joy. "Goose bumps? What a goof! Maybe they were *goof* bumps!" She stood up and waved her arms. "Look at me, Sandi," she said, teasing. "I'm a ghost. Do I scare you?"

"Only when I look at your face!" I snapped.

This time the class laughed at Bobbi Joy. Bobbi Joy scowled, which caused her freckled cheeks to wrinkle up in a menacing way. Her green eyes flashed angrily as she stared at me. Her frizzy red hair seemed to stand straight out from her head. "Sandi Daniels," she threatened, "you're going to pay for that!"

I made a face at her and shrugged. A lot of kids in school were afraid of her, but I wasn't one of them. Neither was Randi.

"Sit down, Bobbi Joy," Miss Morgan ordered. Then Miss Morgan turned to look at me. "And as for you, Sandi Daniels," she said, "the next time I catch

you writing letters in class, you don't stand a ghost of a chance of escaping without an after-school detention." She dropped the letter back on my desk.

"Yes, ma'am," I muttered. "I'm sorry. It won't happen again."

"Good," she replied as she started to walk back to her desk. Halfway up the aisle she stopped to look back at me. Then she smiled and winked. "Do your letter writing during lunch and send Jamie my regards," she said. I smiled back at her and nodded as I stuffed the half-written letter back into my folder.

"Miss Morgan," Chris Miles called out, "do you think ghosts really exist?"

"No way, dude!" Bobbi Joy blurted out. "There are no ghosts."

"Ghosts do exist," Todd Jackson disagreed.

"What do you think, Miss Morgan?" Randi asked.

Miss Morgan sat down behind her desk. The room was silent. Everyone was waiting to hear her answer.

"Well, . . . I think ghosts *might* exist," she said, much to the surprise of Bobbi Joy Boikin.

"I told you so," Todd Jackson announced proudly.

"That's just my opinion," Miss Morgan clarified. "My opinion doesn't prove or disprove the existence of ghosts."

"HA!" scoffed Bobbi Joy. She turned to look back at Randi and me. Randi brushed a strand of blond hair out of her blue eyes and stuck her tongue out at Bobbi Joy. I just wrinkled up my nose at her. The Boikin-Daniels Twins feud had been going on since first grade when Bobbi Joy smeared finger paints on my bologna sandwich during snack time.

"Miss Morgan! Miss Morgan!" called Audrey Snyder as she waved her arm wildly in the air. Audrey was the smartest kid in our class—maybe in the entire school.

"Yes, Audrey?" asked Miss Morgan, giving Audrey a chance to speak.

"When I was doing research about our town for my essay, I discovered some interesting but strange facts about the Morgan Family Mansion," Audrey said. She paused for effect and grinned from ear to ear. I looked at Randi. She shrugged her shoulders as if to say, "What's with Audrey?"

Everyone in school knew about the old Morgan Mansion that stood high on a hill outside of town. The Morgans had once been the richest and most influential family in the area. Somehow they had lost their entire fortune and the mansion had become run-down over the years. Now it was just a scary, old, deserted house owned by Miss Morgan and her brother.

Finally, Audrey stopped grinning and continued. "Isn't the Morgan Mansion haunted by the ghost of one of your ancestors?" Audrey asked our teacher.

"The Morgan Mansion is h-h-haunted?" I gasped in astonishment.

"Yes, Audrey. At least I believe it is," Miss Morgan said without a moment's hesitation.

"I knew it!" Audrey said.

"There's a real ghost in the Morgan Mansion?" Todd asked. "Awesome!"

"Baloney!" Bobbi Joy said.

"Is it baloney?" Randi asked Miss Morgan.

"No," Miss Morgan answered. "The story of the haunted Morgan Mansion isn't baloney. It's a legend about a ghost who cannot rest in peace." Miss Morgan looked around the class and studied each face. All eyes were on her. "If you sit quietly, I'll tell you a haunting tale about one of my ancestors," she said to us. "This is the sad story of Michael Morgan, the ghost of the Morgan Mansion."

I gulped and sat straight up in my chair. I could already feel the goose bumps forming on my skin.

CHAPTER TWO

I T was so quiet in our classroom you'd have thought we were taking a test. "My great-great-grandfather, Martin J. Morgan, made the family fortune by publishing books long, long ago," Miss Morgan began. "He used part of his great wealth to build the mansion that stands outside of town and to fill it with books of all kinds."

"Is that why the historical society wants to use the house as a historical library?" Bobbi Joy called out.

"Stop interrupting!" Randi ordered.

"Yeah. Shhh!" Todd Jackson said to Bobbi Joy.

Miss Morgan waited for us to quiet down. "My brother Jason and I would like to donate the mansion to the historical society for use as a library and a museum, but the building is in such bad shape that it may not be possible," she said in response to Bobbi Joy's question. "The cost of repairing the mansion may be more than the cost of constructing a new building."

"How did the mansion get so run-down if your great-great-grandfather was so rich?" Chris Miles asked.

"That's all part of the ghost story," Miss Morgan explained.

"And we'd hear the ghost story if we'd let Miss Morgan continue," I remarked impatiently.

"Tell us about the ghost, Miss Morgan," Todd Jackson urged.

"Supposedly, it's the restless ghost of Michael Morgan, the oldest son of Martin J. Morgan," Miss Morgan said. "My great-great-grandfather wanted Michael to take over the family business, but Michael wanted to be a sailor and see the world."

"Cool!" Todd Jackson exclaimed.

Miss Morgan continued. "Michael ran away from

home when he was eighteen years old and signed on to a ship named *Petty Theft*. During a violent storm the *Petty Theft* sank and all hands on board were reported lost. When news of the disaster reached my great-great-grandfather, it broke his heart."

"I can understand why," I muttered. "Losing someone you care very much about can seem like the end of the world." I was thinking about Jamie leaving town.

"That's true, Sandi," Miss Morgan said. "Martin J. Morgan soon became seriously ill. He refused to believe that his son was lost forever. He used all of his money to send out ships to search for traces of Michael."

"How sad," said Audrey Snyder. "Did the ships ever find anything?"

"Yes," Miss Morgan replied. "The story continues that Michael was rescued from an uncharted island where pirates had once buried their treasure."

"Pirates? Wow! This story is getting better and better," Todd said as he looked around excitedly.

Then all of a sudden he belched loudly. Everyone laughed. Todd Jackson had a habit of always making rude noises in public. "Excuse me," he said.

"Did Mr. Morgan ever get well again?" Randi asked.

"Tell us more about the pirate treasure!" begged Chris Miles.

Miss Morgan raised her hands to calm the class. "Sadly, Martin J. Morgan died before he learned that his son had been found and rescued," she said. "While Michael was stranded on the island, he found a buried treasure. He brought the chest of pirate loot home with him to the Morgan Mansion."

Bobby Joy Boikin sighed loudly. "Ghosts? Pirates? Treasure chests? What's next—a curse?" she asked sarcastically.

"What *did* happen next?" I asked. I really wanted to know about Michael Morgan. There was something about his story and the Morgan legend that really touched me. I couldn't explain it.

"Michael returned home to the empty mansion," continued Miss Morgan. "Instead of spending his pirate gold, he hid the treasure somewhere in the house and never spent any of it. He lived like a poor hermit, alone in the mansion for a few years. Then one night during a severe thunderstorm, he lost his footing on the stairs and fell down the main staircase. The fall broke his neck. He died there all alone."

I felt a sudden chill that made me shiver. It was the same kind of shiver I felt whenever I saw a spider. Spiders always gave me the creeps.

"How awful!" I cried. "What a tragic tale."

"Right!" said Bobbi Joy Boikin. "And now his ghost haunts the Morgan Mansion? Give me a break!"

"That is exactly what the legend claims," Audrey replied without waiting to be recognized by Miss Morgan. "Michael Morgan is doomed to haunt his father's house until the lost treasure is found and the family fortune is restored."

Miss Morgan chuckled. "Of course, no one knows if there really *is* a treasure," she said. "Many of my relatives have looked for it and no one has ever found it."

"Have any of your relatives ever seen the ghost?" Randi asked.

"Have *you* ever seen the ghost?" I quickly added.

"An aunt of mine claims she saw the ghost once, but I never have," Miss Morgan answered. "My brother Jason and I used to look for the ghost and hunt for the treasure when we were children."

Just then Todd Jackson jumped up. "I just want to say . . . BURP!" He let loose with a massive belch that sounded like a volcanic eruption. We all burst out laughing, even Miss Morgan. "Excuse me again. I just want to say I believe in the legend," he said and then sat down.

Right then, the lunch bell rang. We all got up to leave for the cafeteria. "Ghosts! Pirate treasure! What a bunch of garbage!" Bobbi Joy said, as she picked up her brown-bag lunch and headed toward the door.

"Hurry up, slow poke," Randi said to me as our classmates started to file into the hall. I collected my stuff and followed my sister toward the front.

"I believe in the legend, too," I said to Miss Morgan. "And I'd like to know more about the haunted mansion."

Miss Morgan smiled. "Maybe we can talk about it at your house later tonight," she said. "Your mom phoned this morning and invited me to dinner. Afterwards, we're having a short meeting to discuss the possibility of repairing the mansion so it can be used as a library and a museum."

"That would be great," I answered. I walked out of the room and joined my sister in the hall. "Mom and Miss Morgan are having a meeting at our house tonight," I said to my sister.

"Fine with me," said Randi. "I just hope Mrs. Boikin isn't coming. She always brings Bobbi Joy along." Mom was president of the historical society and Mrs. Boikin was vice-president.

Randi and I got in line for the walk to the cafeteria. "I can't wait to get to the lunchroom so I can finish my letter to Jamie," I said to Randi. "I'm going to tell her all about the haunted mansion and the Morgan legend."

CHAPTER **Three**

D INNER at the Daniels' house is never a thing of
beauty, thanks to my little brother Teddy. He
usually manages to spill something, break something, or knock something over before or during a
meal. Mom claims he's just going through a clumsy
stage known as the Terrible Threes. I wouldn't mind
so much if we hadn't already suffered through a
stage called the Terrible Twos with Teddy.
Sometimes I wonder if the Frightful Fours is next.

However, that night was the exception to the
rule. Teddy was a perfect little helper as we got
ready for Miss Morgan's visit. It wasn't like we went
to a lot of trouble or anything. Miss Morgan had
been to our house many times before. Mom was

making her special meatloaf, which really wasn't all that special. Teddy helped Randi and me set the table without any mishaps.

"Sandi, bring the salad bowl to the table and toss the salad, please," Mom called to me from the kitchen.

"Okay, Mom," I answered.

"Randi, take this pitcher of iced tea into the dining room, please," Dad called. Dad was in the kitchen with Mom helping her get dinner ready.

"Right, Dad," Randi replied. She fell in step behind me as I headed for the kitchen.

"I wanna help some more," Teddy said.

"You can help by sitting at the table and being quiet," Randi said to Trouble. "Miss Morgan will be here any minute." She turned Teddy around and gave him a gentle shove in the direction of his chair.

"I wanna toss salad," Teddy grumbled as he reluctantly flopped his behind down in his chair.

Randi and I returned in a jiffy with the salad and the iced tea. "Don't forget to toss the salad," Mom reminded me. I heard the oven door bang open and I knew Mom was checking on her special meatloaf. I put the salad bowl, which was stuffed high with lettuce, carrots, tomatoes, olives, and other veggies, on the table near Teddy. I picked up the utensils to toss the salad.

Just then the doorbell rang. "That's Miss Morgan," I said, putting down the utensils. "I'll get it."

"You toss the salad," Randi said. "I'll get the door." She started toward the front door. I started after her.

"I said *I'd* get it," I repeated. Randi nudged me. I nudged her back. We pushed and shoved our way toward the front door, arguing over who would answer the bell.

"Fine," I finally said, stopping two steps from the front door. "You get it. I don't want to now!"

Randi stopped dead in her tracks beside me. She folded her arms across her chest and studied my face as the doorbell rang again. "Fine," she said. "If you don't want to get it, then I don't want to get it either. Let it ring." She stubbornly spun around and stomped out of the foyer.

"HA!" I said, chuckling to myself. "That trick works every time." I reached out and opened the door.

"Hi, Sandi!" said Miss Morgan.

"Come in, Miss Morgan," I invited. "I'm glad you're here. I can't wait to hear more about that scary legend." Miss Morgan smiled as I shut the door behind her. I was just putting her things down when I heard my sister shriek.

"Teddy Daniels! Stop that right now!" she yelled.

I looked at Miss Morgan. She looked at me. I bolted toward the dining room without saying a word. Miss Morgan followed. We reached the dining room at the same instant my parents did. Hiding behind a chair on one side of the table was my sister Randi. Standing on a chair on the other side of the table was Trouble. Pieces of lettuce, tomato, onion, and other veggies were flying everywhere.

"Duck!" Randi yelled to us as Teddy scooped some veggies out of the salad bowl and let them fly in all directions. A piece of tomato sailed back over Teddy's shoulder and landed right on Dad's head.

"I tossin' da salad!" Teddy shouted happily. "I tossin' da salad!"

Teddy didn't mean any harm. He just didn't understand what it meant to toss a salad. I looked at Mom and Dad who were both too astonished to utter a word. Dad's face was so red I thought that a slice of tomato was going to fry right on his forehead.

"Theodore Daniels, you're in big trouble," Dad finally said.

Teddy dropped a handful of vegetables back into the almost-empty salad bowl and turned to look behind him. "I toss da salad, dat's all," he said innocently. Dad sighed loudly and wiped the tomato off his face with his hand.

"Teddy tossed the salad," Randi said to Miss Morgan and me.

"Well, Marge," Mom said to Miss Morgan, "I hope you like tossed salad with your meatloaf."

Miss Morgan laughed as she picked a leaf of lettuce off the floor. "It sounds delicious," she said, joking.

Dad lifted Teddy off his chair.

"I toss it far," Teddy said.

"You sure did, Pee Wee," Dad said. He wasn't mad anymore. "Now help us clean it up," he told Teddy.

"I'll help, too," Miss Morgan offered. She looked at Teddy and winked. We all pitched in and began to gather up the raw veggies Teddy had flung around the dining room.

After we'd finished, we sat down to a meal of Mom's special meatloaf, mashed potatoes, and lima beans. I loved lima beans. Randi hated them. Randi stuffed as many lima beans as she could under her leftover potatoes, hoping she wouldn't have to eat any of them.

"Stop trying to hide your lima beans," Mom said to her.

Miss Morgan snickered. "My brother Jason used to do the same thing, Randi," she said.

"I'd like to meet Jason someday, Marge," Mom said. "It's so generous of both of you to donate the mansion to the historical society."

"I just hope we can clean and repair the place enough to make it a worthwhile donation, Shelly," Miss Morgan answered.

"I'm sure it will turn out just right. I wish I could thank your brother Jason face to face," Mom said.

"You'll get the chance to do just that!" Miss Morgan said. "I recently heard from Jason. His company transferred him back to town. In fact, his wife Judy and the kids have moved into an apartment here to house-hunt. Jason stayed behind to clear up some business."

"How wonderful!" Mom exclaimed. "We'll have to have your brother and his family over for dinner."

"Just don't serve him any lima beans," Randi said, joking. She held up a fork with a bean stuck to it. We all laughed.

A short time later, we all finished eating. Randi never did eat her lima beans. "Let's have coffee and dessert in the living room," Dad suggested. "Girls, you clear the table while I get the cake and coffee."

"We having cake for dessert," Teddy said as he hopped off his chair. "Choc-it cake."

"Choc-it cake is my favorite," Miss Morgan told Teddy as she rose from her chair. Mom led Miss Morgan into the living room as Dad headed for the kitchen to get the goodies.

"You go with Mom," I told Teddy. He didn't need any convincing. He scooted off after Mom and Miss Morgan. "Let's hurry and clear the plates," I said to Randi. "I want to ask Miss Morgan about the ghost."

"Why didn't you do that at dinner?" Randi asked as we began to collect dirty dishes. "I know you're bursting at the seams to learn more about that haunted mansion."

"Miss Morgan was talking about other things and I didn't want to be rude," I explained. "Now hurry up and help me."

Randi and I cleared the table in record time. When we went into the living room, Mom had our dessert ready and waiting. Teddy had already devoured his dessert. Most of the chocolate frosting on his cake was now smeared all over his face.

"Girls, I have some interesting news," Mom announced as she handed us plates with big slices of chocolate cake on them. "We're going to have a special clean-up party at the Morgan Mansion."

"A what?" asked Randi with a puzzled voice.

"Well, sort of a weekend sleepover and cleanup," Mom explained. "Miss Morgan and I thought it would be a good idea if we spent a weekend at the mansion and did some hard-core cleaning. We can clean during the days and spend the evenings playing games or something," Mom said. "It'll be fun. I'm sure Mrs. Boikin and Bobbi Joy will want to come, too."

"What?" asked Randi. "Spend a weekend sleeping at a haunted mansion with Bobbi Joy Boikin? Oh, right! That'll be real fun!" she said sarcastically.

"Haunted mansion?" muttered Dad. He took a sip of coffee from his cup. "What's this about a haunted mansion?"

"The Morgan Mansion is haunted by the ghost of Michael Morgan," I blurted out before anyone else could speak. "And there's a pirate treasure hidden there, too!"

Mom and Dad lowered their coffee cups. I covered my open mouth with my right hand and turned to look at Miss Morgan. Then Mom and Dad looked at her.

"It's the Morgan family legend," Miss Morgan explained.

"I've heard about it," Mom admitted. "Didn't the oldest son of Martin Morgan run off to sea or something like that?" she asked. "And didn't he have a tragic accident after he returned?"

Miss Morgan nodded.

"Tell Mom and Dad the ghost story," I urged Miss Morgan.

"Yes," said Dad. "I've never heard of the legend. Tell us about it."

"Okay," agreed Miss Morgan. She smiled and began to tell the story Randi and I had heard in class earlier that day. When she finished, Dad whistled softly.

"That's some family legend," he stated. "The part about the ghost of Michael Morgan is pretty scary."

Just then Teddy jumped off the sofa. He raised

his arms in the air and started racing around the living room. "BOO-O-O-O!" he howled. "I a ghostie! I a ghostie!"

"Stop that, Teddy!" Mom ordered. "There is no such thing as a ghost."

"I don't know about that," Dad disagreed.

"I believe in ghosts, Mom," I admitted meekly.

"BOO-O-O!" cried Teddy as he continued to race around. "I a ghostie!"

"You're a little boy, not a ghostie," Mom said as she corralled Teddy in her arms.

"Does this mean the sleepover clean-up thing is canceled?" Randi wanted to know.

"Of course not," Mom said. "Even a haunted mansion needs a good cleaning once in a while."

"Hooray!" cheered Teddy.

"Calm down, little ghostie," Dad said. "You're not going. You're going to stay home with me." Teddy frowned when he heard that.

"Speaking of *home*," said Miss Morgan, "it's time for me to get going. I have a million things to do now that my brother is moving back to town." Miss

Morgan looked at Mom and then Dad. "Thanks for dinner," she said.

"It was our pleasure," Mom replied. "I'll speak to Cindy Lou Boikin about cleaning the mansion. I'm sure she and Bobbi Joy will lend us a hand."

"Oh, I'm sure they will," Randi grumbled under her breath to me. "If anyone can scare away a ghost, Bobbi Joy Boikin can."

I thought about the ghost. Would I be frightened if I saw it? No, I didn't think so. The only thing in the world that really terrified me was spiders. I knew it was a silly fear, but I just couldn't overcome it. Suddenly, I felt a tap on my shoulder. I stopped daydreaming and turned around.

"BOO!" Teddy shrieked at the top of his lungs. I jumped back in surprise. "I a ghostie!" Teddy cried.

Randi laughed out loud.

CHAPTER **Four**

THE next few days all I could think and talk about was our upcoming sleepover at the haunted mansion. I couldn't wait to explore the scary, old place. I was so excited that Dad let me call Jamie Collins to tell her all about the ghostly adventure that was in store for Randi and me. Jamie said she wished she could go with us and then told me to watch out for the ghost.

"I wonder what a real ghost looks like," I said to Randi as we walked to school the next Thursday. "Do you think you can see through a ghost? I mean, I wonder if ghosts are transparent?"

"Will you stop driving me nuts?" Randi begged. "All this ghost talk is making me batty." She stopped to adjust the shoulder straps on her red backpack.

Red was Randi's favorite color. She even owned a pair of red sneakers, which she just happened to be wearing. I stopped to wait for her and glanced toward the student drop-off area in front of the school. That's when I first saw the boy of my dreams.

He was getting out of a cool sports car. He looked as if he was about my age. I didn't know who he was, but I sure wanted to find out as soon as possible. He was tall and had reddish-brown hair that was cut in a cool style. He wore wire-rimmed glasses, faded jeans, and a blue college sweater. While Randi fixed her backpack, I stood there dumbfounded, gawking at the new boy.

"What's your problem, Sandi?" Randi asked when she finished. "Did you see a ghost?"

"H-he's gorgeous!" I blurted out pointing at the boy who was now walking toward the main entrance of the school.

Randi strained her eyes to get a good look at

40

him. "*Him?*" she remarked, befuddled. "No way. He's okay, but he's not as cute as Wormy Wormley or Eric St. John." These were two boys she'd had crushes on in the past. "In fact, I think he looks kind of average."

"Average!" I sputtered angrily. "Randi Daniels! How any twin sister of mine can say something like that about a boy as cute as that boy is beyond me!" I sighed and watched as the boy went into our school.

Randi shrugged her shoulders. "I guess he's a new student," she said, ignoring my outburst. "I'm glad you think he's so gorgeous. Maybe now you'll stop thinking about ghosts all the time." She smirked at me and started toward the entrance.

"What do you mean?" I asked as I trailed after her.

Randi looked back over her shoulder and grinned. "I mean," she said, "maybe you'll stop thinking about ghosts . . . now that you're in love!" She laughed, threw open the door, and dashed into school.

"Randi Daniels, you take that back!" I demanded. I yanked the door open and raced in after my sister. "Take that back or else!" I threatened as I started chasing her down the hall.

"Slow down, ladies," Miss Morgan ordered as we bolted around a corner. "I know you can't wait to get to my class," she said, joking, "but running in the halls is against school rules."

"Yes, Miss Morgan," Randi replied sweetly. She slowed to a walk instantly. She grinned at me and went into our classroom.

"Sorry, Miss Morgan," I apologized. I flashed her a grin and followed Randi into the room. We quickly put our stuff away and sat down.

"I was only kidding, Sandi," Randi apologized as I settled in behind my desk and waited for the bell to ring. "That new boy is sort of cute, but he is definitely not my type."

I smiled at her. I could never stay angry at Randi for long. It was like being mad at myself.

Besides, Randi wasn't only my twin. She was also my best friend.

"If you think that boy is so cute," Randi continued, "introduce yourself to him at lunch. If he's a fifth-grader, he'll be in our lunch period."

She was right. Our school had three fifth-grade classes. All of them had the same lunch period. I guessed that if the new boy was a fifth-grader, he'd probably be put in Mr. Windor's or Mrs. Gold's class. Both of those fifth-grade classes had fewer students than our class.

"Of course," Randi whispered, "we could be wrong."

"Wrong?" I asked. "What do you mean?"

"Maybe he's only a third grader who's big for his age," Randi explained.

"Very funny!" I said. Leave it to Randi to say something like that and ruin my beautiful, romantic daydream. The bell rang. Miss Morgan walked into the room and shut the door behind her.

"We'll just have to wait until lunch time to find out for sure," Randi whispered as Miss Morgan began reading the morning announcements.

It seemed like an eternity until lunch. I almost

jumped out of my seat when the bell finally rang.

"What's the big hurry?" Bobbi Joy asked Randi while I pulled my sister toward the open doorway.

"Sandi can't wait to try a new sandwich our mom made her for lunch," Randi said, teasing. "It's a peanut butter and sardine sandwich."

"UGH!" said Bobbi Joy.

"Come on, Randi!" I urged. "Hurry up!" I took Randi by the arm and yanked her out into the hall.

"Peanut butter and sardine sandwiches always make me belch," Todd Jackson said to Bobbi Joy.

"Everything makes you belch," Audrey Snyder said as she strolled by Todd and Bobbi Joy.

"Do you think Todd ever really ate a peanut butter and sardine sandwich?" Randi asked me.

"Who cares?" I answered as we started for the lunchroom. "I'm on a mission. I've got to find out about you-know-who."

Randi placed her right hand over her heart. "Ah, yes! Mr. Wonderful!" she said as we entered the cafeteria.

I walked in a short way and then scanned the tables searching for a trace of the new boy. "Th-there he is!" I said to Randi. I pointed out the boy we'd seen this morning. He was standing in the hot-lunch line with his back to us. "See?" I asked. "This proves he's in fifth grade."

Randi grabbed my lunch bag out of my hands. "Well, go up and introduce yourself," she told me. "Pretend you're the welcome wagon. Tell him 'hi' from the friendly Daniels family." She gave me a little shove with her free hand. I staggered forward a step or two and then froze. I felt paralyzed. My legs refused to work. I couldn't budge. I stood there stiffly, glued to the floor.

"Is anything wrong, Sandi?" Chris Miles asked as he and several of our classmates walked by, heading for the lunch line.

"Did you suddenly lose your taste for peanut butter and sardine sandwiches?" Bobbi Joy asked as she went past.

"If you don't want it, I'll eat it," said Todd

45

Jackson. He walked over and got in the lunch line.

"I-I can't do it, Randi," I sputtered. I spun on my heels and bolted back out into the hall. I turned the corner and went directly into the nearby girls' restroom.

"Hey, Sandi! Wait!" Randi called as she chased after me holding both of our lunch bags. She came into the restroom and found me staring blankly into the mirror.

"I-I can't go up to him," I explained to my sister. "I'm too nervous. I've never felt like this before. I totally chickened out."

"Wow! You must think that guy is really something!" Randi said. She put our lunch bags on the shelf below the mirror. "But how are you ever going to get to know him if you don't introduce yourself? You have to talk to him sometime."

I sighed. "I will . . . eventually. I just wish there was some way I could find out a few things about him without actually talking to him myself." Suddenly, a brilliant idea popped into my head. I slowly turned and stared into my sister's eyes. "I know a way I can do it! A way *we* can do it!"

"We?" Randi asked, scratching her head as if she was confused. "What do you mean *we?*" Then her eyes popped open wide. "No! Not the old switcheroo?"

I nodded. "Yes! The old Daniels Twins' Switcheroo!" I said as I brought my face closer to my sister's until the tips of our noses almost touched.

"No way, Sandi!" Randi refused as she backed up and raised her hands. "I won't do it. Every time we trade places, we get into trouble—deep trouble."

I folded my arms stubbornly across my chest. "How many times have I helped you out by pretending to be Randi Daniels?" I asked. Randi gulped. She knew the answer—plenty of times. "You owe me big time, Randi," I continued. "Now it's payback time. All you have to do is trade places with me for a few minutes. Go up to the new boy and introduce yourself as sweet, lovable Sandi Daniels."

47

"Oh, brother!" groaned Randi. She smacked her forehead with her hand.

"Introduce yourself and find out all you can about him," I instructed. "Once I know some things about him, I won't feel so nervous about talking to him the next time. It's as simple as that."

"The old switcheroo is never simple," Randi reminded me. "Nine out of ten times, it backfires."

"Not this time it won't," I assured her. I took off my glasses and put them on her face. "Of course, it would have been easier if I had worn my contacts today instead of my glasses," I said.

I had on my favorite pink sweater, a short, plaid skirt, and black flats. Randi was wearing her old Washington Redskins football jersey, jeans, and her red basketball sneakers.

"Love sure makes people do weird things," Randi sighed as she untied her sneakers.

"Thanks, Randi," I said as I began to take off my sweater. "Thanks a million."

"What's a twin sister for?" Randi asked. She handed me her sneakers.

It didn't take long to swap clothes. Minutes later, Randi and I left the restroom dressed as each other. On the way to the cafeteria, we passed Chris Miles who was getting a drink from the water fountain in the hall.

"Are you okay now, Sandi?" he asked Randi. "You looked really strange in the cafeteria a little while ago." He never suspected he was talking to the wrong twin.

Randi glanced at me. I winked back at her. "I'm fine, Chris," Randi said. "Thanks."

We went into the lunchroom. Just inside the door, we stopped to look for the new boy. I spotted him as he was getting up from a table to carry his tray to a nearby trash bin.

"There!" I said to Randi as I nudged her in the ribs with my elbow. "He's going to dump his leftovers into the garbage." The boy was moving toward the same trash can where Bobbi Joy Boikin was already clearing her tray. "Go to it, Sandi Daniels," I said to my sister.

"Right, Randi Daniels," she replied.

Randi sure looks good in my pink sweater, I thought as my sister walked straight toward the new boy. I held my breath as the distance between them shortened to a step or two. *It's going to work,* I thought. *The old switcheroo is going to work out just fine.*

Then something just awful happened. Randi stepped in a small puddle of spilled milk and slipped.

"EEEK!" she screamed as she smacked right into the new boy. His tray went hurtling out of his hand and landed on the floor with a loud crash. Everything on the tray went flying, too. Empty milk cartons sailed through the air and showered down onto the cafeteria floor. The boy's plate of leftover spaghetti plopped into the trash can, but not before a splash of tomato sauce splattered right onto my favorite sweater. Last, and worst of all, a catapulted apple core went skyward and conked Bobbi Joy Boikin right on the noggin.

Randi gulped and cried loudly, "Excuse me!" In a panic she spun around and streaked toward

me like a bolt of lightning covered with spaghetti sauce.

"Sandi Daniels, you big clumsy klutz!" Bobbi Joy Boikin roared as Randi and I ran out into the hall.

"Let's get out of here!" Randi said. We both hurried away from the disaster scene.

"I knew the old switcheroo wouldn't work!" she said after we had stopped running.

"You were right," I said, sniffing sadly.

We walked back to the restroom to swap clothes once again. I knew I didn't stand a chance of making a good impression on that new boy now.

CHAPTER **Five**

RANDI and I spent the rest of the lunch period hiding out in the girls' restroom. While in there, I tried, without success, to wash the spaghetti sauce stain off my sweater. Not only had Randi messed up my chance to meet the new boy, but she had also ruined my favorite sweater.

"I'll have to apologize to him, Randi," I said to my sister. "It's the only thing to do. I'll just walk right up to him and apologize."

"I tried to warn you about trading places," Randi said as she finished off the last bite of her peanut butter and strawberry jam sandwich. I had the same kind of sandwich. It might as well have been a peanut butter and sardine sandwich as far as I was concerned. I was too upset to enjoy my food.

"The accident really wasn't my fault," my sister said. "I couldn't help bumping into him."

"I know," I said, relieving Randi of any feelings of guilt. "It was all my fault. I should have bumped into him myself." Randi and I looked at each other and burst out laughing.

"If he's the type who holds a grudge over a silly little accident, then he's not worth knowing—no matter how handsome you think he is," Randi said.

"Right," I agreed. "Absolutely. I just hope Bobbi Joy Boikin isn't the type who holds a grudge over a silly little accident."

A big grin appeared on Randi's face. "Did you see that apple core bop her?" she asked. "Wham! It smacked her right on the head."

"At least nothing was broken. There was no real harm done," I added.

"Except to your sweater," Randi reminded me.

Suddenly, the bell to return to class rang. We tossed our trash in the waste basket and hurried out into the hall. At the door to our classroom Miss Morgan was talking to Bobbi Joy. Bobbi Joy saw us coming. She pointed at us, said something to Miss Morgan, and then went into the room.

"Uh-oh," groaned Randi. "It looks like Miss Apple-head spilled the beans about what happened at lunch." We walked slowly toward Miss Morgan.

"Just a minute, Sandi," Miss Morgan ordered. I stopped outside the room. Randi kept walking. "You, too, Randi," Miss Morgan said. Randi gulped and halted. She backed up beside me. "Sandi," began Miss Morgan, "did you hit Bobbi Joy on the head with an apple core?"

"Uhh . . .," I said, sputtering. "In a way . . . I guess I did. But I didn't mean to. It was a dreadful accident."

"Yeah. A dreadful accident!" Randi repeated. "Sandi was . . . uh . . . daydreaming about ghosts and she bumped into someone. An apple core went flying off his tray and hit Bobbi Joy."

"That's right," I quickly agreed.

"Even though it wasn't on purpose, I want you

to apologize to Bobbi Joy immediately," Miss Morgan said.

"Yes, ma'am," I replied. Randi and I started into the classroom.

"And," Miss Morgan added, "I want to see both of you after school today, so make sure you stay behind after class." We sighed and then nodded solemnly.

"Great," Randi whispered to me. "I have to stay after school now because of what you did."

"Me?" I whispered back. "You did it!"

"But I was you," Randi said, glaring at me as she walked to her desk. I took a deep breath and walked up to Bobbi Joy Boikin.

"I'm sorry about what happened at lunch time, Bobbi Joy," I said.

"You should be," Bobbi Joy snapped. "Try not to be so clumsy next time. If I was that new boy, I'd have gone straight to the principal and complained about you."

My mouth dropped open in shock. Maybe that was why Miss Morgan had ordered Randi and me to stay after school. Maybe we were in trouble with the principal. I thought terrible thoughts as I went to my desk. In my mind, I saw the new boy pointing me out to the principal and shouting, "That's the one! She's the klutz who knocked the tray out of my hands!"

"What's wrong now?" Randi asked as I sat down across from her. "You're as pale as a ghost."

"Nothing is wrong," I lied. "I guess my lunch didn't agree with me."

"That's what you get for eating peanut butter and sardine sandwiches," she said, teasing.

That was just like my sister. One minute she was angry and the next minute she was joking. Sometimes I wished I could be more like her and not let things bother me so much. But, of course, I wasn't at all like Randi.

I worried the rest of the day. I was still brooding over Bobbi Joy's remarks when the dismissal bell rang. As everyone else gathered up their things and left the classroom, Randi and I remained seated at our desks.

"This won't take long," Miss Morgan said to us as she got out of her chair. She walked toward the exit. Turning, she said, "Don't look so nervous you two. Relax." Then she walked out of the classroom.

"Great," Randi said as she slouched in her chair. "Where do you suppose she went?"

"To get the principal," I said.

Randi sat up straight instantly. "The principal!" she gasped. "What for?"

"You'll see," I predicted grimly. We heard footsteps approaching the room. In walked Miss Morgan followed by the new boy.

"Randi and Sandi Daniels," said Miss Morgan, "I'd like you to meet my nephew Michael Jason Morgan—we call him M.J. for short."

"I wish I was a ghost," I whispered to Randi, "because I'd disappear right now."

I sank as far down in my seat as I could. Randi hid her face with her hands. After an instant, Randi uncovered her face, grinned sheepishly, and waved to the new boy.

"Uh . . . hi . . . M.J.," Randi said. "I'm Randi."

She pointed at me. "That's my twin sister Sandi. I think you've already met her."

I was so embarrassed that I tried to slide even lower in my seat. I slid so far down I fell off the chair and tumbled awkwardly into the aisle. I smiled feebly from the floor and waved to Miss Morgan's nephew.

M.J.'s eyes narrowed to slits as he stared at me sprawled on the floor. "Oh, yes," he said. "How could I ever forget Sandi?"

"Oh, did you and Sandi already meet?" Miss Morgan asked M.J.

"Not really," M.J. explained. "We sort of bumped into each other at lunch."

"Good!" said Miss Morgan.

"Not so good," I muttered under my breath as I got to my feet. I decided it was time to grab the bull by the horns. I motioned to Randi and together we went up to shake hands with M.J. Despite what had happened at lunch, he seemed friendly enough.

"That's a cool football jersey," M.J. said to Randi as they shook hands. "Do you like football?"

Randi shrugged her shoulders. "It's okay," she said. "I like soccer better. I'm a goalie on the school team."

"Awesome!" M.J. exclaimed. "I think soccer is great."

"I-I like soccer, too," I said nervously as I shook M.J.'s hand.

"That's nice," he said matter-of-factly.

"I'm really happy you two hit it off so nicely," Miss Morgan said to M.J. and me.

M.J. winked at me. "Sandi did all the hitting," he said, kidding.

"That's for sure," Randi agreed.

"Will you be going to school here now?" I asked, trying to shift the subject away from the lunchroom disaster.

"Yes," Miss Morgan answered for M.J. "That's why I wanted you to meet each other. I thought the Daniels twins would be just the right students to show M.J. the ropes at our school."

"It would be our pressure—I mean, pleasure—to show him the ropes," I said nervously.

Randi laughed. "It sounds like Sandi's ropes are a bit tongue-tied," she said, teasing.

"Would you mind showing me the ropes, too, Randi?" M.J. asked my sister. His eyes seemed to twinkle when he looked at her.

"Sure," Randi answered. "It will be my pressure."

M.J. laughed.

"M.J. and his mother are going to help with our cleanup at the mansion this weekend," Miss Morgan told us.

"Aren't you afraid of the ghost?" Randi asked him.

"If you're talking about the Morgan legend," answered M.J., "it doesn't bother me one bit. In fact, I was named after the ghost himself. And I sure wouldn't mind finding his lost treasure."

"Me either," Randi agreed.

"Well, I'd like to help free the ghost of Michael Morgan," I said. "If finding the treasure will help him to rest in peace at last, then I'm all for finding it, too."

"Spoken like a true romantic," Miss Morgan complimented. "If the ghost is listening to this conversation, he knows he has a friend in Sandi Daniels."

"Yeah," agreed Randi. "My sister Sandi, a ghost's best friend." She and M.J. chuckled. I gave Randi an angry look.

"You girls better head for home before your mom starts to worry about you," Miss Morgan said.

"It was nice meeting you, Randi," M.J. said. After a brief hesitation he added, "Oh, and you, too, Sandi. I'm looking forward to this weekend at the mansion."

"I'm sure it'll be fun," I replied.

"I guess," Randi agreed. We went back to our desks and collected our things.

"Bye, Miss Morgan," I said. "Bye, M.J."

"So long," M.J. called to me. "See ya, Randi."

"Tell your mom I'll be in touch with her about this weekend," Miss Morgan said to Randi and me as we walked out of the room.

I sighed. "M.J. is so handsome," I said after we

were in the hallway.

"He is pretty nice for someone who's not my type," Randi said. "He didn't even tell his aunt about what happened at lunch."

"I know," I answered. I looked at the spaghetti sauce stain on my blouse. "Every time I look at this stain, I'll think of him."

"How can a glob of tomato sauce remind you of a boy?" Randi asked.

"You have to be a romantic at heart to understand," I told her.

We went out through the back exit of the school and started walking home. "Sandi," Randi said, "how can we be so alike in some ways and so different in others?"

"I don't know," I answered. "But I do know that different or alike, we always stick together."

"Absolutely," Randi answered. "The Daniels twins stick together no matter what." She raised her hand and we exchanged high-fives. "Maybe this cleanup thing at the haunted mansion won't be so bad after all," Randi said. "It might be real fun."

As we approached our house, I glanced over at Randi. "I just wish Bobbi Joy and Mrs. Boikin weren't going to be there," I said. We started up the walk to our front door.

"It could be worse," Randi answered. "Mom could be bringing Trouble along. Thank goodness Dad is going to baby-sit Teddy this weekend."

I opened the front door. Trouble was running around raising a ruckus. "I a ghost ruster!" he was shouting. "I a ghost ruster!"

Mom was about to carry Dad's empty suitcase upstairs. "What's he yelling about?" Randi asked Mom, as I closed the front door.

"He's been carrying on like that ever since I told him he's going to the Morgan Mansion this week-end," Mom explained.

"What?!" I cried. "But Dad is supposed to be baby-sitting Teddy this weekend!"

"I a ghost ruster!" Trouble bellowed as he ran in circles flapping his arms like a big bird.

"Your father has to take a business trip this weekend," Mom explained. "It's a last-minute thing.

Teddy will have to come with us." Mom looked at us and shrugged. "Don't worry. He'll behave himself."

"Right," Randi muttered.

Mom started up the stairs with Dad's suitcase.

"I a ghost ruster!" Teddy repeated as he ran up to Randi and me.

"That's ghost *buster!*" I corrected him.

"Some weekend this is going to be," Randi said groaning. "Ghosts! Bobby Joy Boikin! And now Trouble, too! What's next?"

I thought about the haunted mansion. Suddenly, a strange feeling came over me. I felt goose bumps forming on my arms.

"Who knows?" I said to Randi. "Who knows?"

CHAPTER **Six**

RAIN pelted our car on all sides as we drove to the Morgan Mansion on Friday night. The rumbling thunder was so loud it actually made the car shake. The most frightening part of the storm wasn't the ceaseless rain or the loud thunder. It was the crackling lightning that streaked across the night sky, time after time after time.

"Dis is cool!" Teddy exclaimed as the brilliance from the latest flash of lightning faded from view.

"Right," groaned Randi. "This is a perfect night to visit a haunted mansion."

Randi was with Mom in the front seat of our station wagon. Trouble and I were buckled up in the back seat. Stored behind us in the rear of our

67

station wagon were all types of cleaning gear and our overnight stuff, which included sleeping bags and my makeup case. I never went anywhere without it.

"I hope this thunderstorm lets up soon," Randi said just as thunder rumbled and lightning flashed again.

"The storm is supposed to last until way past midnight," I told my sister. "Mom," I said, "do you think the Morgans and the Boikins are already at the mansion?"

Mom didn't answer right away. She was concentrating on the road ahead. Driving through a rainstorm out in the country where there were no street lights wasn't easy. "Miss Morgan said she and her sister-in-law Judy were leaving for the mansion right after school let out," Mom finally answered. "So, I guess Marge and Judy and the kids are already there. I don't know about Cindy Lou and Bobbi Joy. Maybe this terrible weather has slowed them down."

Suddenly, something Mom had said sunk in.

"Mom, . . . did you say *kids* when you mentioned the Morgans?" I asked.

"Yes, *kids*," Mom replied. "M.J. and little Annie."

"M.J. has a sister?" Randi asked. "We didn't know that."

"He never mentioned a sister to us when we ate lunch with him today," I said.

"Did you girls tell M.J. about your little brother Teddy?" Mom asked.

A long steady rumble of thunder shook the car again. "WHE-E-E!" cheered Teddy gleefully.

"Well, no," I confessed. "I guess we forgot to mention him."

"Well, maybe M.J. forgot to mention his little sister Annie," Mom explained. "Marge told me about her. Annie is three years old just like Teddy."

"Don't tell me she's going through the Terrible Threes, too," Randi said.

"She's probably a sweet little girl," I said before Mom could answer. "I can't wait to meet her and I can't wait until we get to the mansion."

"That figures," Randi said to me. "This is like a

vacation for you. You're spending the weekend with Mr. Wonderful and you might even get to see a real ghost."

"I da ghostie!" Teddy yelled. He pounded his fists on the car seat and hollered, "BOO-O-O-O!"

"Stop that, Teddy!" Mom ordered. Teddy immediately ceased his pounding and booing.

"I might consider it a vacation if Bobbi Joy decided to stay home," I remarked.

Mom flicked on her bright lights and made a right-hand turn off the highway onto a narrow private lane. The lane wound around some large spruce trees and led up to the Morgan Mansion.

"Sorry, girls," Mom said. "It looks as if your vacation plans are over. There are two cars parked in front of the mansion and one of them belongs to Cindy Lou Boikin."

"Hip, hip, hooray," said Randi, without a bit of enthusiasm.

It was the last thing any of us said as we neared the huge house. I leaned forward and peered over Randi's shoulder to get a better view of the

mansion. It was my first close-up look at the place. We'd driven past it on the main road many times, but groves of tangled trees had always hidden it from view.

The house was constructed of large blocks of stone and it had a slate roof. Three huge chimneys extended skyward like the towers of a medieval castle. Creeping up the outside walls of the mansion were twisted vines of ivy. The mansion itself was completely dark except for a dim light that streamed out of the front windows near the main entrance.

"It doesn't look very inviting in the dark, does it?" Mom asked as she parked behind Mrs. Boikin's car. Thunder rumbled and lightning flashed as if in response to Mom's comment.

"I bet it's real cozy inside," I predicted.

"Dis place is cool!" Teddy cried as he unbuckled his seat belt and reached for the door handle.

"Hold it right there, young man," Mom ordered. At the sound of her voice, Teddy froze. "Everyone grab the sleeping bags and the other things we'll need for tonight so we don't have to come back out in the rain." Mom said. "Sandi, be sure to bring the bag with the flashlights and candles in it. I packed it just in case," she told me.

I took off my seat belt and grabbed the things we'd need to spend the night in the mansion. Of course, I included my makeup case. I passed stuff forward to Mom and Randi.

Randi patted the bundle containing the flashlights and candles. "I sure hope we don't have to use these," she said.

"In a storm like this, who knows?" Mom replied. "The electricity could go out at any time."

"Great!" Randi muttered. "Just great!"

"Does someone have the food?" Mom asked.

"Yup!" I replied. "It's right here." I held up the canvas bags containing the food we'd brought along.

Mom reached for the car door handle. "The rain has let up a little. When we get out, let's make a mad dash for the front door," she said. "Teddy, you take my hand."

"Dis is fun," Teddy said.

"Let's go!" Mom said.

We threw open the car doors, jumped out into the rain, slammed the doors shut, and raced for the Morgan Mansion. Before we reached the doors, they opened, and there stood Miss Morgan with an umbrella in hand. Just behind her I could see M.J. and Bobbi Joy peering out into the stormy night.

"Hurry in or you'll get soaked!" Miss Morgan called. "I was just coming out to meet you!"

Mom dashed into the foyer of the mansion and pulled Teddy in behind her. Randi scooted in next and I followed. We had used the bags we were carrying to shield us from the rain, so we were a little wet, but not soaked.

"What a night!" Miss Morgan exclaimed as she shut the door behind us.

"Welcome to the Morgan Mansion," M.J. said as we dropped our gear on the floor.

I didn't answer. A weird feeling came over me. I felt strangely attracted to the old house. Goose bumps formed on my flesh as I studied the inside of the mansion. Dangling from the ceiling was a large, dusty chandelier covered with cobwebs. Several of its light bulbs were out. The weak light it gave off filled the foyer with an eerie glow. On the walls were large, old paintings of faraway landscapes and people dressed in old-fashioned clothes. Pieces of antique furniture were covered with sheets that had long ago turned yellow with age.

The one thing that captured most of my attention was the large main staircase in the rear of the foyer leading to the dark upper floor. It had a beautiful banister, even though some of the spindles were missing or broken. I just knew it was the staircase from the legend—the one Michael Morgan had fallen down long ago. Looking at it made me shiver.

"So, how do you like the haunted mansion?" Bobbi Joy asked me. The sound of her raspy voice snapped me out of the spell I'd fallen under.

"Sandi, are you okay?" Miss Morgan asked. "I don't think you've heard a word anyone has said since you came in the door."

"Huh? . . . What?" I sputtered.

Before I could utter another sound an ear-piercing scream echoed from a nearby room. Randi and I jumped and turned toward the shocking sound. A little girl with long, brown hair tied up in pigtails came running into the foyer followed by Mrs. Boikin and another woman.

"I a pie rat!" yelled the little girl. "I a pie rat's ghostie!" she shrieked again. She stopped short when she spied Teddy.

"Who is that?" Randi whispered.

"That," explained M.J., "is my little sister Annie. I call her Little Awful Annie because she's such a pest."

"I a ghostie, too!" Teddy suddenly hollered as if taking his cue from Little Awful Annie. He began to chase Annie around and around the foyer.

"That's our little brother Teddy," I said to M.J. "His nickname is Trouble and I'm sure you can guess why."

"Teddy!" called Mom.

"Annie!" said M.J.'s mother.

Miss Morgan chuckled. "Oh, let them burn up some energy," she suggested. "They can't hurt anything."

Mom and M.J.'s mother laughed. "I guess when you're three years old, introductions aren't important," Mom said.

"Marge has told me so much about you and the twins. I feel like we're all old friends," M.J.'s mother said. "I'm Judy Morgan." She shook hands with Mom and Randi and me as Miss Morgan introduced us to her sister-in-law.

"I get you, pie rat," Teddy called as he chased Annie back toward the main staircase.

"You can't get me, Mr. Ghostie!" Annie shouted as she bolted down a hallway leading to the rear of the house.

Before anyone could stop them, Teddy and Annie raced down the hallway and were out of sight. Mom and Judy raced after them.

The thunder boomed louder than ever and lightning flashed through the windows. Suddenly, the chandelier flickered, dimmed, and then went out. The entire mansion was completely dark.

"Wh-what happened?" Bobbi Joy cried.

"It must be a power failure," said Miss Morgan.

"Where are Teddy and Annie?" Mom asked anxiously.

"I don't hear them," Judy answered. She sounded worried. "Annie!" she called. "Annie! Can you hear me?"

"E-e-e-e-k!" we heard Annie cry. "Mommy, I a-scared!"

"Teddy!" I yelled. "Teddy! Where are you?"

"I dun know!" Teddy cried out. He didn't sound very close.

"We're coming, kids!" Mom yelled. "Don't move! The lights will be on soon!"

"I hope so," Bobbi Joy muttered.

"I brought four flashlights," Mom said.

"They're in this bag, Mom," I answered as I reached down to the bundle at my feet. I unzipped the side of the canvas bag and stuck my hand in. I felt around and pulled out a flashlight and clicked it on. I pulled out the other flashlights and clicked them on. Mom took the first one and then handed the next two to Mrs. Boikin and Miss Morgan. The last flashlight I kept for myself.

"I think we should split up to search for the kids," Miss Morgan suggested. She shined her light to the left of the foyer. "Shelly and I will look down that hall. Judy and M.J., you look down there," she said, pointing in the opposite direction.

"What about us?" Mrs. Boikin asked.

"I think it would be a good idea if you stayed here with the three girls, Cindy Lou," Miss Morgan said to Mrs. Boikin.

"That sounds good to me," Bobbi Joy mumbled.

"We want to search too, Mom!" I pleaded.

"Yeah!" agreed Randi. "We're worried about Teddy!" Even though Teddy bugged us most of the time, Randi and I loved him very much.

"Well, . . .," Mom said, "okay. But don't stray far from the foyer."

"I'll be waiting right here if anyone needs me," Mrs. Boikin volunteered.

Randi and I watched Mom and Miss Morgan go off to the left and M.J. and his mom go off to the right.

"What's in there?" I asked Mrs. Boikin. I shined

my flashlight toward the room she'd come out of when we'd first entered the mansion.

"That's the library," Mrs. Boikin answered. "Marge said it's the biggest room in the mansion."

"We'll look around in there," I said. "Come on Randi." I started toward the dark entrance to the library.

"Not so fast," Randi said as she tugged on my shirt. "Slow down."

"Teddy?" I called. "Annie? Are you guys in there?" I ventured into the dark, shadowy library with the flashlight clenched in my shaking hand and my nervous sister creeping along behind me.

CHAPTER **Seven**

THE library was filled with dusty furniture. Most of it was covered with large, yellowed sheets. Built into the walls were bookcases that stretched from the floor to the ceiling. The shelves were stocked with thousands of books of all colors and sizes.

"This room is totally scary," Randi said.

"It's totally awesome," I answered as I admired the wondrous stacks of books. The beam of my flashlight lit an area filled with two couches, a few chairs, and a large table that were all uncovered. Piled nearby were packages, bags, and suitcases. "That must be everybody's gear," I said.

"Yeah," Randi replied.

We walked slowly toward the uncovered furniture. Just beyond was a huge fireplace. It was so big it took up an entire side of the room. Moving closer to it, I noticed a large painting hanging over the mantle. Slowly, I raised my flashlight until it illuminated the painting. It was the portrait of a young man, probably in his twenties. He was posed before the very same fireplace. He had a handsome face with a square jaw and bright, blue eyes. His hair was dark, not quite black, but darker than regular brown. Instantly, Randi and I knew just who it was.

"It's him," Randi whispered. "It's the ghost. It's Michael Morgan." She stepped back away from me.

I stood perfectly still. I couldn't take my eyes off the painting. The portrait was so realistic it seemed to be alive. Strangely, I had the feeling it was telling me something. I took a step closer to the mantle and shined the light directly onto the face of Michael Morgan. I could have sworn that the face in the picture was smiling at me—ever so slightly. I smiled back. All of a sudden, Randi and I heard an eerie moan that turned our blood to ice.

"Oo-oo-oo-oo-ooh!" someone or something groaned from the shadows behind us.

"The ghost is in this room!" Randi shrieked. She dropped to the floor and scrambled behind a huge, high-back chair positioned near the wall where the fireplace met the bookcase. She left me alone to face whatever was behind us.

Slowly I turned. The flashlight twitched in my hand as the beam sifted through the shadows.

"Oo-oo-ooh!" came an anguished cry from the dark. My knees knocked together as I shined the light on a white shape rising up from the floor near the cluster of uncovered furniture. I blinked my eyes in astonishment.

"Sandi Daniels!" rasped the ghostly shape. It was hard to see in the large, dark room. "Answer me!" it moaned.

I gulped. "Y-yes?" I sputtered. "I-I'm not afraid of you. I want to help you."

"Oo-oo-oo-ooh! Sure you do!" the ghost replied sarcastically.

Just then, the electricity came back on. I found myself talking to someone hiding under a white sheet that had obviously been taken from a nearby piece of furniture. It didn't take a genius to figure out who was under that sheet.

"Ha! Ha! I sure frightened you!" Bobbi Joy Boikin howled with laughter, as she pulled off the sheet. "You were both scared stiff!"

"We were not!" Randi grumbled as she crawled out from her hiding place.

"That was a dirty, rotten trick, Bobbi Joy," I said angrily.

"That evens the score for hitting me on the head with an apple core," Bobbi Joy replied.

"How'd you like a hit over the head with a flashlight?" I said.

"Mom! Mom!" yelled Bobbi Joy, smirking. "Come quick! Sandi is about to freak out!" Mrs. Boikin came rushing into the room, followed by Miss Morgan, M.J., Judy, and our mom. Teddy and Annie trailed behind them.

"You found them!" I exclaimed. I forgot all about

Bobbi Joy and I ran up to Teddy. I gave him a big hug.

"Where did you go, Teddy?" Randi asked him. "We were worried about you."

"We wuz playin' ghostie," Teddy answered.

"So was I," Bobbi Joy said, chuckling. Randi and I gave Bobbi Joy double dirty looks.

"The sky went boom!" Annie exclaimed. "It got dark!" As if on cue, thunder rumbled and lightning blazed.

"The power could go out again at any time," Mom predicted.

"I agree," Miss Morgan said. "So, tonight, let's limit our exploring to the nearest bathroom, which is at the top of the stairs, and to the rooms off the foyer. I also suggest we move our sleeping bags into the foyer and sleep there tonight. It's the best-lit room in the mansion."

"And no more running around the mansion," Mrs. Morgan said to Annie.

"That goes double for you, Trouble," I said to Teddy.

"I brought plenty of peanut butter, jelly, and bread," Mom said. "We can make sandwiches and play games."

"I have chips and popcorn," Miss Morgan added. "And Judy brought soda."

"I have a thermos of hot cocoa," said Mrs. Boikin, "and a box of doughnuts. We can have a real pig-out picnic in the foyer."

"Too bad you guys didn't bring any courage with you," Bobbi Joy whispered to Randi and me. "We could go ghost hunting after everyone falls asleep." She snickered and began collecting her belongings from the pile in the library.

"Don't let Bobbi Joy bug you," M.J. said. "Down deep, she's the biggest chicken here." He picked up his sleeping bag. I started to help with the gear when Randi pulled me aside.

"I found something!" Randi whispered in my ear.

"What?" I replied softly.

"I accidentally discovered a secret passageway while I was hiding behind that chair!" she said.

"A secret—" I started to say, but before I could

finish, Randi clamped a hand over my mouth.

"Do you girls want something?" Mrs. Boikin asked. She was the only one in the library now, besides Randi and me.

"No, ma'am," Randi said as she removed her hand from my face. "Sandi just has the hiccups."

"Oh, that's too bad," Mrs. Boikin said. "Maybe a good fright will cure them." She picked up her bags and went out into the foyer, leaving us alone.

"Where is it?" I asked Randi.

"Over there, where the fireplace wall meets the wood of the bookcase," Randi explained. She led the way.

As I walked past the painting of Michael Morgan, I looked up and smiled at him again. He still seemed to be smiling right back at me.

"Down here!" Randi said. She pulled me down behind the high-backed chair.

"Where?" I asked as I plopped down beside her. "I don't see anything." I looked and looked at the wall, but all I could see were the fieldstone rocks of the fireplace and some slats of wood that covered a small rectangular space between the rocks and the bookcase.

"Watch this," Randi said. "I accidentally pressed against this stone when I was hiding back here." She placed her hand on a round rock that stuck out from the fireplace wall just a bit further than the others. She pushed against the rock and it gave way ever so slightly. The wooden slats covering the rectangular space rose slowly to reveal a dark passageway in the wall.

"Let me have the flashlight," Randi ordered. I handed it to her. She clicked it on and shined the beam into the passageway.

"Yuk!" I gasped as I looked inside. It was narrow and crowded with spider webs.

"I wonder where it goes?" Randi asked.

I shrugged my shoulders. "Maybe we should tell Miss Morgan about it," I said.

"Miss Morgan said to limit our exploring to the downstairs rooms," Randi reminded me. "This room is downstairs. So let's explore."

"You're awful brave all of a sudden," I said.

"What's gotten into you?"

"Bobbi Joy's prank proved to me how silly it is to be afraid of something that doesn't exist," Randi said. "Besides, I'd like to find that treasure." She crawled into the secret passageway and stood up, brushing aside spider webs. "Come on," she beckoned. "Follow me."

"No way!" I said. "Spider webs mean one thing: spiders. You know how I feel about spiders." I shivered. "I'm staying right here."

"Suit yourself," Randi shrugged. "I'll find the treasure myself." She started down the secret passageway before I could stop her.

"Randi!" I whispered, poking my head into the passageway. "Randi! Come back! We should stay together!"

"I'll be fine!" she whispered back. She turned a corner and disappeared from sight.

I sat there and stared anxiously into the black passageway, looking for my sister. Maybe it was my imagination, but I thought I saw something strange. It looked like drifting smoke or mist. It was swirling around slowly in the middle of the passageway. It seemed to be taking on the shape of a person. I watched in awe as what looked like a face slowly appeared. At that very instant, light from Randi's flashlight flooded the passageway again. The misty form quickly vanished.

"I'm back," Randi announced as she turned the corner and came into sight. "I followed the passageway to the end. No treasure." She bent over and came out of the passageway.

"Yuck! Look at you!" I said. Randi was covered with spider webs from head to toe. "Ick!" I exclaimed. "There's a big spider in your hair!"

Randi tried frantically to brush it off. The spider fell to the ground and dashed back into the passageway disappearing into the darkness.

I didn't bother telling Randi about the mist I'd seen during her absence. I knew she wouldn't believe a word of it anyway.

"Where does the passage go?" I asked.

"Around the corner, it splits into two passageways," Randi explained. She paused to clear more spider webs from her clothing. "One passage-way goes to a study on the other side of the foyer. There's a secret door there, behind a huge desk. The room is filled with model ships and old sailor stuff."

I wondered to myself if it was the study of Michael Morgan. "Where does the other passageway lead?" I asked.

"It goes to a secret stairway that leads up to the hallway on the second floor," Randi said. "A wall panel in the hallway up there is really a trap door."

"Cool!" I said.

"I'll tell you what's really cool," Randi answered. She pressed the stone that closed the door to the secret passageway. We stood up. "While I was treas-ure hunting, I figured out a way to get even with Bobbi Joy for scaring us."

"How?" I asked as we came out from behind the chair.

"When everyone falls asleep tonight, I'll wake up Bobbi Joy and dare her to go ghost hunting," Randi began. "You refuse to go along and say that you're going into the library to get a book to read instead.

You're such a book nut she won't suspect anything."

"Right. Go on," I urged.

"While you're in the library, I'll lead Bobbi Joy into the study," Randi continued.

"Okay. Go on," I said again.

"You put on a white sheet and use the secret passageway to go into the study. When you appear in the study as a ghost, Bobbi Joy will freak out! She won't suspect it's a trick because she'll think you're still in the library!"

"Hold it right there," I said to my sister. "It's a great plan, but it has one big flaw."

"Flaw? What flaw?" Randi asked.

"The passageway," I replied. "It's full of spiders, remember? I'm not going in there. Not even to scare Bobbi Joy Boikin."

We walked slowly toward the middle of the room. "That is a problem," Randi admitted. "I could go into the library instead of you," she said, "but I'd need a good excuse. Bobbi Joy knows I'm not a big reader."

"Maybe you could pretend you forgot something in here," I suggested.

"That might work," Randi answered. "But Bobbi Joy is the suspicious type. She might smell a rat. The book thing would work better."

I stopped and looked at my sister. "We already fooled Bobbi Joy once this week with the old switch-eroo, so why not twice?" I asked. "Why don't you be me for tonight?" I said.

Randi's eyes opened wide. "Yeah! The old switch-eroo again!" she exclaimed. "Of course! It's just what we need to pull off the perfect prank. We can swap clothes in the bathroom before we go to bed and no one will ever know!"

I nodded. "Speaking of changing clothes," I began, "mine are still kind of damp from the rain. Let's change into something that will be easier to switch later."

"Good thinking, Sis," Randi answered.

At that moment Mom appeared in the doorway.

"What are you girls doing in here?" Mom asked.

Randi glanced at me hoping for an explanation. We couldn't tell Mom that we were plotting ghostly revenge against Bobbi Joy. I looked at the portrait of

Michael Morgan hanging over the fireplace. "We were just admiring the painting, Mom," I answered. "It's such a sad story."

"It certainly is," Mom agreed, staring up at the painting. "He was very handsome," she said. "It's a shame he died so tragically and at such a young age." Mom looked at Randi and me. All of a sudden, she grabbed us both and hugged us. "Okay, you two. Stop dawdling. Come into the foyer and get something to eat. And hurry up before the Morgan ghost gets you," she said, teasing, as she ushered us out of the room.

Randi winked at me. "He's going to get someone later tonight," Randi predicted. Luckily, Mom didn't hear her. As we walked away I thought about the mist I'd seen in the secret passageway. The face that had started to form had looked a little like the face in the painting. It made me wonder.

CHAPTER **Eight**

"Do you have to bring your makeup case with you everywhere you go?" Randi asked me. I turned away from my reflection in the mirror to look at my sister who was behind me in the bathroom.

"A young woman should always be prepared to look her best," I told her.

"Oh, right! I forgot. Mr. Wonderful is downstairs!" Randi said, teasing.

I ignored her and closed the lid of the makeup case and put it aside. "Did we come up here to gossip about my love life or to swap clothes?" I asked.

"Don't be so touchy," Randi answered. She unzipped the top of her red jogging suit and took it off.

I did the same with the top of my pink jogging suit. We were both wearing sweat pants so the transformation of identities was swift and easy.

"I wish you'd wear your contacts more often," Randi said as I handed her my glasses. She put them on and studied her looks in the bathroom mirror. "Perfect," she said. "In this dim light, I'll even be able to fool Mom."

"Do you think they're still telling scary stories downstairs?" I asked Randi.

"Probably," she answered. "Mrs. Morgan's story about Big Foot and the lost campers was pretty neat."

"I liked her tale about the aliens from outer space who came to Earth to clone people," I said.

"Who needs to be cloned when all you have to do is to pull the old switcheroo?" Randi said, joking. She pulled me close so both of our reflections showed in the mirror. "Okay, Randi," she said calling me by her name. "It's payback time for Bobbi Joy."

I nodded. "I just hope it doesn't take too long for

everyone to fall asleep," I said.

The storm was still raging. Thunder boomed and the lights in the upstairs bathroom flickered.

"Let's go," Randi said.

"Right," I replied.

We walked out into the hallway just as the thunder rumbled again. Walking the short distance to the main staircase, we began to go down slowly into the foyer, step by step by step. I swallowed hard. I couldn't help thinking about Michael Morgan's fatal fall down those stairs. A deep sadness came over me. Randi seemed to sense it.

"Are you okay, Sandi?" she asked as I stopped half way down. "Is anything wrong?"

I shook my head. "I'm not sure," I replied. "This place makes me feel strange. It's almost like someone or something is trying to tell me something." I sighed heavily. "Come on. Let's hurry," I urged, as we began to hear the sound of voices below.

"It's about time," Mom said when she saw us at the bottom of the stairs. A sleepy Teddy was cradled in her arms. Mom and Teddy were both parked on

Mom's sleeping bag. Judy was next to them with Annie asleep on her lap.

"We thought Bigfoot got you two," M.J. said, kidding.

"I thought they were abducted by aliens," Bobbi Joy said, joking. She was sprawled out on her sleeping bag.

I didn't want to say too much. Fooling Mom with my looks was one thing, but tricking her with my speech was another. There was a slight chance Mom might recognize me and ruin our plan. I kept my sentences short and sweet.

"Do you believe in them?" I asked Bobbi Joy quietly, as I sat down beside her. Randi and I had placed our sleeping bags between Mom and the Boikins.

Bobbi Joy glared at me. "No, I don't believe in ghosts, Bigfoot, or aliens," she snapped.

"We'll see," Randi whispered to me.

"I tired!" Teddy yelled out suddenly. Everyone giggled.

"I tired, too," Miss Morgan agreed. "I think we've

told enough scary stories for one night."

Mom yawned. "We've got a lot of work to do tomorrow," she said. She and Teddy lay down and eased into their sleeping bags.

"Good night, all," Mrs. Boikin said. "I sure hope I can fall asleep with the lights on and with all that racket going on outside." She and Bobbi Joy lay back and closed their eyes.

"Good night, Randi," M.J. said to me. "See you tomorrow. Goodnight, Sandi," he said to my sister. Randi winked at me. We had everyone really fooled.

"Good night," I replied. I slipped into my sleeping bag and settled in to wait for the others to fall asleep.

Before long, a loud snoring echoed through the foyer. It was Mrs. Boikin. The noise didn't seem to disturb anyone else, because it was partially drowned out by rumbles of thunder outside.

"She's a regular buzz saw," Randi whispered to me. "Staying awake is easy when you're next to her!"

"It doesn't seem to bother Bobbi Joy any," I whispered back. We glanced at Bobbi Joy. She was dozing peacefully next to her mom. "Do you think they're all sound asleep?"

Randi shrugged. We both sat up and looked around.

"I guess everyone was really tired," I said. "It didn't take long for them to conk out."

"Okay, let's put our plan into action," Randi said. "I'll lie back down. You wake up Bobbi Joy."

I nodded. After Randi was flat on the floor, I reached over and tapped Bobbi Joy on the shoulder. She wriggled a little, but didn't wake up. I tapped again, this time harder.

Bobbi Joy shot up into a sitting position like she had been catapulted off the floor. Her eyelids snapped open. "I'm up, Mom. I'm up. I won't be late for school," she mumbled. Then she turned and looked at me through dazed eyes. A scowl formed on her face.

"What's the big idea, Randi?" she grumbled.

"Shhhh!" I said, quieting her. "I just thought you'd like to prove you don't believe in ghosts," I told her.

"Wh-what's going on?" Randi muttered. She sat up and rubbed her eyes as if she'd been sleeping. She yawned and slipped my glasses on. Everything was going just as we'd planned.

"Bobbi Joy and I are going ghost hunting," I said to my sister. I looked at Bobbi Joy. "That is . . . unless she's chicken."

"Who's ch-chicken?" Bobbi Joy asked.

"Good," I said. "Let's take a look in there." I pointed to the study. "I think that used to be Michael Morgan's study. If the ghost is anywhere tonight, I'll bet he's in there."

"I've heard enough of this," Randi said. "Thanks to you two, now I'm wide awake."

"Aren't you coming ghost hunting with us?" I asked my sister. Of course, I already knew what her response would be.

"No, thanks," Randi answered. "But since I can't sleep now, I might as well find a good book to read." Randi picked up one of the two flashlights near us and got to her feet. Without saying another word, she walked away from us and into the library.

"That leaves just us," I said to Bobbi Joy. I picked up the other flashlight.

"I don't know about this," Bobbi Joy protested. "It's late and I'm tired."

"Do I have to start making chicken noises?" I asked. Bobbi Joy frowned.

"Okay, Randi," she whispered as she got to her feet. "We'll see who's chicken."

I smiled and stood up beside Bobbi Joy. With the index finger of my right hand, I beckoned for her to follow me. I held the flashlight in my left hand and crept quietly toward the closed, double doors of the study. Bobbi Joy was so close behind me I could feel her breath on my neck. I paused at the door to the study. I wanted to be certain that Randi had enough time to get from the library to the study through the secret passageway.

"Now, keep your eyes peeled for the ghost," I instructed.

Bobbi Joy made a sour face in response. I put my hand on the doorknob and turned it. The hinges squeaked a little as I pushed the door open. Light from the foyer seeped into the dark study. I clicked on the flashlight and used it to survey the room. It was filled with sailing mementos and artifacts, just like Randi had described earlier.

"See? There's nothing in here except some old sailing junk," Bobbi Joy grunted. We walked further and stopped in the middle of the room. I moved the flashlight's beam from one side to the other. "This is a waste of time, Randi," Bobbi Joy said. "Sandi was smart not to come with us." When the flashlight beam passed the huge desk in the room, a blob of white rose up from behind the desk moaning loudly.

"GAH!" yelled Bobbi Joy. "Look! A ghost! YEOW! The ghost is after me!" she shrieked. In a fit of fright, she spun on her heels and ran for the door, flapping her arms in the air like a wounded bird.

"Help! Help! The ghost is after me!" she hollered.

Randi and I almost laughed our heads off. Randi pulled off the sheet she had on and tossed it onto a nearby chair.

"That was the funniest thing I ever saw!" she said, laughing. She handed me my glasses and I

put them on.

"It sure was," I agreed. At that moment I happened to look up toward the ceiling. Much to my amazement, the white mist that I'd seen earlier in the secret passageway was now hovering above our heads! It was whirling and swirling like a ghostly tornado.

"R-Randi!" I gasped. "L-look at that!" I pointed upward.

"What?" she asked. She looked where I was looking. "I don't see anything," she said. The mist started taking on the shape of a person again.

"You don't see that?" I asked, directing her chin with my free hand.

"All I see is the ceiling," Randi insisted. "But I see trouble ahead if we don't hurry and switch clothes before someone sees us!" She began taking off my pink jogging jacket. It was obvious she didn't see whatever was floating around there on the ceiling. I watched silently as the smoky mist disappeared.

"Hurry! Give me my jacket!" Randi urged. She

handed me my jacket and I took off hers. Suddenly, we heard a commotion coming from the foyer. We quickly zipped up our jogging jackets and walked toward the door.

"Bobbi Joy sure flew out of here like a chicken with its tail on fire," Randi said, chuckling.

I nodded. The big smirks on our faces faded as soon as we walked into the foyer and saw everyone glaring at us. Bobbi Joy was trembling from head to toe and clinging to her mother like a huge piece of Scotch tape.

"In-in there," Bobbi Joy said as she pointed frantically to the study. "The ghost was in there! Randi and I saw . . ." Bobbi Joy's voice trailed off as she realized that Randi and I were now both together. "Hey! Wait a minute," she cried.

"What's going on, girls?" Mom demanded. She was holding Teddy who was trying to blink the sleep out of his eyes. "Bobbi Joy ran in here shouting that she and Randi had seen a ghost."

"Bobbi Joy knows there are no such things as ghosts," Randi replied.

"She *did* say that," M.J. added. He looked at Randi and me and winked. Then he turned to help his mom with Annie who was now also awake.

"Where da ghostie?" Teddy mumbled. "I wanna see da ghostie!"

"I think we've all seen and heard enough about ghosts for one night," Miss Morgan said.

"Well, I think you girls pulled a nasty prank on my Bobbi Joy," Mrs. Boikin accused. She gave Randi and me a dirty look.

"You mean like the sneaky stunt Bobbi Joy pulled on the girls earlier when we were hunting for the children, Cindy Lou?" Mom asked.

Mrs. Boikin cleared her throat nervously. She knew Mom was right. "It's time to end all of these silly pranks," Mrs. Boikin stated. "We're here for an important reason."

"Absolutely," Miss Morgan said. She looked at Bobbi Joy and then at us. "How about it, girls?"

"Yes, ma'am," Randi and I agreed in unison.

"Okay," Bobbi Joy said. She gave us both the evil eye. "I wasn't really afraid," she added.

"I could tell that by the way you flew in here," M.J. said sarcastically. Everyone chuckled, including Mrs. Boikin.

"How did you get from there to there?" Bobbi Joy asked me. She pointed from the library to the study.

"I'll explain all about it in the morning," I replied.

"You've both got a lot of explaining to do in the morning," Mom said to Randi and me. We recognized the stern look on Mom's face. It was her no-nonsense-I-mean-business look.

"At least the old switcheroo worked out without a hitch," Randi whispered in my ear.

I nodded.

"What was that?" Mom asked us as everyone settled back down in their sleeping bags for the night.

"Oh, nothing, Mom," I said. I put my flashlight down near my sleeping bag. It was then that I noticed my makeup case was missing. I'd left it up in the bathroom when Randi and I had switched jackets.

"You two had better stay put for the rest of the

night," Mom said.

"I will," Randi promised. She flopped down on her sleeping bag.

"I will, too," I said. "Just as soon as I get my makeup case."

CHAPTER **Nine**

I LOOKED into the bathroom mirror and yawned. After adjusting my glasses, which had slipped down the bridge of my nose, I thought about the prank we'd pulled on Bobbi Joy. It made me laugh out loud. The way she'd reacted proved that down deep she believed in ghosts as much as I did, but she just refused to admit it. I picked up my make-up case and headed for the door.

At the door I stopped and yawned again. I was really exhausted. I lifted the door latch and stepped out into the hall. My tired eyelids sprung up like tightly wound shades after a tug at the bottom. I swallowed hard. Not ten feet away from me in the middle of the hall was the haunting mist I'd seen twice before. It was swirling around and around. I stood in a trance as the mist took on the shape of a person: arms, legs, a body, and a head all began to appear. I recognized who it was instantly. It was the person I'd seen in the painting hanging over the fireplace in the library. It was the ghost of Michael Morgan.

When the ghost was fully formed, he looked like a regular person except that he was partially transparent. A dim glow surrounded him, like the glow you see around a firefly on a summer night. Strangely enough, I wasn't at all frightened. He looked lonely and seemed to need a friend. I felt so sad for him that I wanted to reach out and give him a big hug. (I didn't, though, because I wasn't sure if a living person could even hug a ghost.)

I think he sensed my feelings. He made no threatening gestures and didn't speak a word. He just smiled at me in a sad way and beckoned for me to follow him. I started after him until I heard a loud commotion coming from the main staircase. Turning away from the ghost, I saw Annie running toward the bathroom followed by her brother, M.J.

"I gotta go bat-room bad!" Annie shouted. She scooted through my open legs, ducked into the bathroom, and slammed the door shut. I looked to see if the ghost was still there. Much to my surprise, he was. M.J. obviously didn't see him, though.

"Sorry, Sandi," M.J. said as he came up to me. "When Little Awful Annie has got to go, she's got to go." He stopped beside me. I looked at M.J. and then glanced at the ghost who was drifting back down the hall away from us without moving its legs. He was sort of skating on air.

"You don't see that?" I asked M.J., pointing in the direction of the ghost.

"Huh?" he asked. "See what?" He looked right at the ghost and acted as if nothing was there. I sighed and shook my head in confusion. Suddenly the ghost became mist again, whirled into a swirling white mass, and then totally vanished.

"What were you saying, Sandi?" M.J. asked.

"Oh, nothing," I replied. "I guess I'm just tired."

I started walking away. I was so confused by what had just happened that I even turned my back on the chance to spend a few minutes alone with M.J.

"If you wait until Annie is finished, we'll all walk down together," M.J. offered.

"That's okay," I said. "I'll see you downstairs." I started down the staircase. I didn't know what to think. Was I seeing things? Was it all in my imagination? Was I the only one able to see the ghost of Morgan Mansion?

When I reached my sleeping bag, I found that Randi was already sound asleep. Judy Morgan was barely awake, waiting for Annie and M.J. to return. I smiled at her. Everyone else was in slumber land. In fact, Mrs. Boikin was already busy sawing another log with her snoring. I put my makeup case on the floor and laid down beside my sister. I was out as soon as I shut my eyes.

Even though I was totally exhausted, my slumber wasn't very restful. I dreamed about the old Morgan Mansion and the sad ghost that haunted its halls. I saw the ghost in my dreams and he spoke to me. "You are my only hope," the ghost said. "Help me. Help free me from this place. I must fulfill my duty to my family so I can rest in peace at long last. Find my treasure and free me, Sandi Daniels."

I heard his words so clearly it was as if I was having a conversation with a friend. "Why me?" I asked. "Why have you chosen me?"

The ghost continued. "Because you aren't afraid," he explained. "You feel compassion for me. Please help me, Sandi."

"I will help you!" I cried out loud. And at that instant, I woke up.

The storm had stopped. Morning was near. I sat up and looked around. Everyone else was still snoozing. I rubbed the sleep from my eyes and put on my glasses. Turning, I looked back over my shoulder at the staircase. The ghost was standing on the last two steps. His right arm was outstretched and pointing toward the library.

"W-wake up, Randi!" I whispered as I poked my sister. "Please wake up!"

"Wh-what?" Randi asked. She rolled over and opened her weary eyes. I pulled her up into a sitting position and directed her attention toward the staircase.

"Tell me you don't see the ghost of Michael Morgan standing right there!" I demanded. The ghost continued to point toward the library.

"Are you nuts?" Randi asked. "I don't see anything. Now let me sleep a little longer!" She flopped back down in a heap. I looked where the ghost had been standing. He was gone. I thought about my disturbing dream. The ghost's words echoed inside my head. "Help me! Find my treasure and free me, Sandi Daniels!"

I shook my head and glanced at Randi, who was now peacefully dozing once again. "I can't find that treasure alone," I muttered to myself. "And I need more than just ghostly help. I have to prove to the ghost he can trust Randi, too." I took a deep breath and sighed heavily.

But first I'd have to prove to Randi that the ghost really did exist.

CHAPTER **Ten**

"SANDI, this bathroom must be your favorite room in the mansion!" Randi said. "You spend more time in here than in any other room. It took you an hour to get dressed in here this morning and all you put on was your purple jogging suit. Now you're dragging me in here."

I glared at my grumpy sister. "At least I'm not wearing the same grungy jacket two days in a row like someone else I know," I snapped. Randi had on the same red jogging jacket she'd worn the night before. Now, she was also wearing the matching red pants that went with it.

"I got dressed in a hurry this morning because I didn't want to miss breakfast," Randi explained. "I still didn't get downstairs fast enough to have any of Mrs. Boikin's leftover doughnuts."

"It wasn't my fault," I said. "Teddy, Annie, and Bobbi Joy wolfed them down before I could save one for you." I looked at my sister. "I didn't bring you here to talk about clothes or who ate the leftover doughnuts."

"Then why did you bring me up here?" Randi asked. "We're supposed to be cleaning the main staircase with M.J. Everyone else is busy cleaning up the mansion. We're the only ones goofing off."

I frowned. "We are not goofing off," I stated. "We have important work to do right here."

"Are you going to lecture me about the ghost again?" she asked. "I told you this morning I think you've been seeing things." Randi gently put her hands on my shoulders and faced me. "There is no ghost. Your eyes have been playing tricks on you."

"Like the one we played on Bobbi Joy?" I replied.

Randi rolled her eyes and threw up her hands. "Please don't remind me about that," she begged.

During breakfast Randi and I had explained

what happened to Bobbi Joy in the study the night before. We told Mom the whole story, including our discovery of the secret passageway. Mom didn't think our prank was very funny. We were lucky to have gotten off with just a stern scolding.

"Randi, I really did see the ghost of Michael Morgan," I told my sister, "and I think I can prove it to you."

"And how can you do that, Miss Ghost Buster?" she asked.

"In the dream I had last night the ghost said that I'm the only one who can see him because I'm the only one who isn't afraid of him."

"What's that got to do with me?" Randi questioned. She began to think about the problem. From the funny look on her face I could tell she knew what I had in mind.

Randi put two and two together and it added up to the old switcheroo. "Oh, no, you don't!" she protested backing away from me. "You brought me up here to switch places, didn't you?" She backed up so far that she bumped right into the closed bathroom door.

"If the ghost thinks you're me, maybe he'll show himself to you," I said to Randi. "Then you'll know I'm not seeing things, and then, maybe the ghost will let us both help him. Together we can find the treasure!"

"No way, Sandi," she protested. "Nope! Absolutely not!"

"Oh, Randi, come on," I pleaded. I unzipped my purple jogging jacket, removed my glasses, and grinned at her. "You're not afraid, are you?" I asked. I held out my jacket and glasses to her.

"Oh . . . okay," she finally agreed, as she took my jacket and glasses. "Do you really think we can pull the old switcheroo on a ghost?"

I shrugged my shoulders. "If I hide in here while you walk around as me, who knows what might happen?" I said. I stopped talking and started to undress. Randi did likewise. We quickly swapped outfits.

"It's getting so you can't tell which Daniels twin is which without a scorecard," Randi muttered a few minutes later. She peered into the bathroom mirror and slipped my glasses on.

"Good luck, Randi, . . . er, I mean, Sandi," I said as I pushed Randi toward the door.

She opened it. I slowly nudged her out into the hall. I kept the door open a crack and peeked out as she started down the hall. When she neared the main staircase, I watched and held my breath. I wondered if our trick would work. Could we fool a ghost with the old switcheroo?

Suddenly, I saw a white mist form out of thin air near Randi. The mist began to trail after her like a lost kitten. Randi didn't know it was behind her. Slowly the mist took the form of the ghost I'd seen and dreamt about the night before.

"It's him," I whispered to myself. "It's the ghost of Michael Morgan. The old switcheroo does work on ghosts! He thinks Randi is me!"

Suddenly, Randi stopped in her tracks. She shivered as if an icy breeze had just blown over her. Slowly she turned to look back at me and at the ghost, too. I could tell by the way her jaw dropped and her eyes opened wide that she saw the ghost at

long last. Randi stood there trembling and pointed right at the ghost.

"Now we can both see ghosts," I whispered.

The ghost of Michael Morgan breezed by Randi and then beckoned with his hand for her to follow him. Randi glanced back in my direction for an instant and then stumbled after him. She followed him obediently as he floated toward the main staircase. I waited for them to drift out of view before I left the bathroom. I tiptoed down the hall and peeked down into the foyer. I saw the ghost leading a startled Randi into the library. Other than Randi and the ghost, the downstairs seemed deserted. Everyone else was probably busy cleaning in different parts of the mansion.

After Randi and the ghost moved into the library, I scooted down the stairs as fast as my feet could carry me. At the bottom of the stairs, I spied M.J. coming out of the study. He closed the door behind him and looked over at me.

"Hey! Just where have you been, Randi?" he asked. "We're supposed to be cleaning the stairs."

I held a finger to my lips and shushed him. "I'm not Randi. I'm Sandi," I said.

M.J. did a double-take. He stared at me and blinked his eyes. "You're Sandi?" he asked. He shook his head slowly in disbelief. "No way," he said. "No way!"

"I am, too," I insisted.

"If you're Sandi, then where is Randi?" he asked.

"She's in the library with the ghost of your ancestor," I said. Before he could say another word, I grabbed M.J.'s hand and pulled him toward the open library door. We stopped just outside the room and peeked inside. I saw the ghost. He was looking at Randi and pointing at a book shelf near the mantle. Apparently, all M.J. saw in the room was Randi dressed in my clothes and wearing my glasses.

"Good goog-a-mooga!" M.J. exclaimed loudly. "Which twin is which?"

At the sound of M.J.'s outburst, the ghost turned to face us. He looked at me. He looked at Randi. Then he looked back at me and then at

Randi again. In a blink, the ghost vanished.

"Sandi! It was him!" Randi shouted excitedly. "It was the ghost! I saw him. He led me in here!"

I raced up to my sister. "I know!" I cried happily. "I watched the whole thing!" We clasped arms and began to bounce up and down together with glee.

"What is going on?" M.J. asked as he walked up scratching his head. "Have you two gone bonkers?"

My sister and I stopped bouncing. Randi handed me my glasses. I put them on. M.J. studied my face. He pointed at me. "You really are Sandi," he said. He turned to Randi. "And . . . you're really Randi?"

Randi nodded. "And we've both seen the ghost of Michael Morgan!" she announced. Randi and I winked at each other.

M.J. was still confused. He shook his head slowly, puzzled. "I didn't see the ghost," he muttered. "Why didn't I see the ghost?"

"It's a long story," I said. "We'll explain later."

Randi nodded. She turned toward the mantle.

"The ghost was trying to show me something over there." She pointed out exactly where.

I walked toward the bookshelf. "Maybe there's a book on that shelf he wants us to see," I said.

"Let's look," Randi answered. Together we grabbed M.J. and pulled him over to the shelves. "Let's get busy," Randi ordered.

One by one we began to pull books off the shelf. "*Alice's Adventures in Wonderland*," I read. "This can't be what he wants us to see." I put the book aside.

"Hey!" said M.J. as he pulled out a dusty, old book. "Here's an old edition of *Treasure Island*." He flipped open the book. To his surprise and ours, the middle of the book was hollowed out. Tucked inside the hollowed-out pages of the book was a small diary.

"Be careful," Randi instructed as M.J. lifted out the diary. He placed the old, worn book down and then opened it to the first page.

I looked at the page and read the words written on it. "'My Days Aboard the Ship *Petty Theft* and the Discovery of the Pirate Treasure . . . by Michael J. Morgan,'" I read. I sighed and looked at M.J. and

Randi. They both gulped.

"It's the ghost's diary," M.J. said.

"Do you know what this means?" Randi asked. "It means that the legend about the treasure is true!"

M.J. nodded his head. "We'd better tell Mom and Aunt Marge about this right away," he proposed. He shut the diary and headed toward the door.

"Wait!" I cried. I grabbed M.J.'s arm and pulled him back. "We'd better not get their hopes up," I said. "Suppose the treasure isn't in the house?"

"It has to be," Randi argued. "That's why the ghost appeared to you."

"I'm not sure of that," I answered. "I think we should look through the diary for more clues before we tell anyone about any of this."

M.J. hesitated. He looked at the diary in his hand. Then he turned and looked me square in the face. "I think you're right, Sandi," he admitted. "I think we should search the diary for clues and I think we should try to find the treasure ourselves."

"Let's go treasure-hunting!" Randi cheered.

CHAPTER **Eleven**

"Not a clue!" M.J. complained as he closed the diary. "There's not a darn clue in here about where the treasure is hidden!"

"But why did the ghost lead me to this book?" Randi asked, puzzled.

"I think I know," I said, thinking of all we had just read. "He wants everyone, especially me, to know more about him. This diary explains why he left home to become a sailor. He wants everyone to know he loved his father and the rest of his family very much. He didn't leave home because he wanted to hurt anyone. He left because it was something he had to do for himself."

M.J. looked at me. "I think Sandi is right," he

said. "I got so caught up in the treasure fever I forgot all about Michael Morgan. I'm ashamed of myself for being so insensitive."

"Sandi is sensitive enough for all three of us," Randi said. She smiled at me. "I guess that's why the ghost chose her to appear to."

"At least the diary is positive proof that the Morgan treasure does exist," I said. "With a little luck maybe we can still find it." I looked at the painting of Michael Morgan over the mantle.

"Luck?" Randi said to me. "What we need is help from your ghostly pal."

I was still looking at the picture when the familiar white mist began to seep out of it. "Look!" I cried as I pointed at the painting. "He's back!" The mist quickly took on the form of Michael Morgan.

"I still don't see anything, Sandi," M.J. said. He stared blankly at the painting.

"I hate to say it," said Randi, "but I don't see anything either."

"Well, I sure do!" I exclaimed. "The ghost is right there!"

"I guess you're still the only one who can see him," Randi said. "I sure hope he's not mad about the old switcheroo. Does he look angry?"

I shook my head. "I think he's here to lead us to the treasure," I said. I stared at the ghost floating above us. "Are you here to guide us to the treasure?" I asked. He slowly nodded. I turned to Randi and M.J. "He's here to help!" I told them.

"I can't see you," M.J. said as he looked up at the ceiling, "but I know you're there. I'm proud to be related to you. I'm going to tell people all about you and get them to read about your adventures. You'll be famous and admired. I promise." A faint smile appeared on the ghost's face.

"He's moving!" I shouted as the ghost floated toward the open door. "He wants us to follow him." I dashed after the ghost and Randi and M.J. followed. We moved through the deserted foyer and paused at the closed doors of the study. The ghost waved his hand and a gust of wind blew the doors wide open. We all moved into the room.

"Hey! What's the big idea?" Bobbi Joy Boikin

yelled as we burst into the study. "Don't you yahoos know enough to knock before you enter a room?"

Randi ignored Bobbi Joy. "Do you see the ghost, Sandi?" Randi asked me. "Is he still here?"

I shook my head. "No," I replied sadly. "He's gone."

"BOO-O-O! I da ghostie!" Teddy yelled as he jumped out from behind a couch in the study.

"I a pie-rat!" Annie shrieked as she tumbled out after Teddy.

"And I'm out of here!" announced Bobbi Joy. She glared at M.J. and headed for the foyer. "When I said I'd watch those two brats while you looked for Sandi and Randi," Bobbi Joy grumbled, "I didn't think you'd be gone so long."

M.J. gulped. "Gee, I'm sorry, Bobbi Joy," he said. "I forgot all about you and the kids." M.J. glanced at Randi and me. "Our moms brought Teddy and Annie down while you were gone," he explained. "We were supposed to be baby-sitting them."

"And I'm supposed to be helping my mom in the

attic," Bobbi Joy said, annoyed. She frowned at us and stormed out of the study. We heard her footsteps stomping up the stairs.

"Pie-rats can't catch ghosties!" Teddy yelled. He began to race around the room.

"You a silly ghostie!" Little Awful Annie bellowed as she joined in the chase. "I get you!"

"Stop that, you two!" I ordered. I grabbed Teddy as he went by and made him stand still. M.J. grabbed his sister. I bent over and looked Teddy square in the eye. "Please do something quiet, Teddy," I pleaded. "We have important work to do in this room."

"Otay, Sanee," Teddy agreed. "I gonna color some pictures."

"I wanna color, too!" Annie said.

"Fine," M.J. said. "Go get your coloring things and come right back."

As soon as we released Teddy and Annie, they bolted into the foyer. "Do you think the treasure is here in this room?" Randi asked as she craned her neck and looked around.

"It must be," M.J. said. I heard Teddy and Annie scoot back into the study. When I turned around again, I couldn't see Teddy, but I saw Annie holding some coloring books.

"Maybe there's a secret passage in here that leads to the treasure," Randi said.

"We gonna color now, Sanee!" Teddy shouted from behind a chair.

"Fine. That's a good boy, Teddy," I answered. I was so busy thinking about the treasure that I wasn't paying any attention to what Teddy and Annie were doing. Randi and M.J. weren't either.

"Well, where should we start to look?" Randi asked me.

I thought for a few minutes. Then I did a slow spin to survey the room. When I turned completely around, I saw Trouble and Little Awful Annie busy at work.

"Teddy!" I yelled angrily. M.J. and Randi both looked behind them.

"Oh, no!" M.J. cried.

"You're not supposed be coloring on the walls!"

Randi hollered at Teddy and Annie.

"And you're not supposed to use lipstick and makeup as crayons!" I shouted. We ran over to stop the two would-be artists, but it was too late. They had made an awful mess.

A wood panel behind the desk was completely smeared with streaks of lipstick and smudges of blush. On the floor near the Terrible Two was my open makeup case.

"I drawin' da ghostie!" Teddy explained as I snatched my lipsticks from his hands. With the help of M.J. and Randi we collected my makeup and put it all back in the makeup case. I slammed the lid of the case closed. I glared at my little brother. He had lip gloss on his forehead and streaks of eyebrow pencil all over his face. Annie had blush on her forehead and big, red circles of lipstick on her cheeks.

"You're both a mess!" I said. I pointed at the wall. "And you've ruined that wall! Now we have to clean this up."

"I guess the treasure hunt will have to wait,"

M.J. said. "I'll get some water to wash off the makeup."

"I'd better wash off these two makeup artists," Randi said. "I'll take them up to the bathroom." She took Teddy and Annie by their hands and led them away. A few seconds after they'd gone, M.J. returned with a pail of soapy water and some sponges.

"It's going to take more than soapy water to clean this," I said. "Believe me, I know. Thanks to Trouble I've had plenty of experience with this type of art."

"I left some liquid cleaner up on the stairs," M.J. said. "I'll go and get it."

While he was gone, I decided to try to wash off some of the blush. I took a sponge out of the bucket and began to scrub the wall as hard as I could. I must have triggered a secret latch because all of a sudden I heard a faint "click" sound and then a rectangular section of the wall swung open like an automatic door.

The secret door was two feet wide and three feet

high. I looked into the passageway that had been revealed in the wall. It was dark and full of creepy cobwebs. I was going to call for M.J. to return but I didn't. Instead, I looked into the passageway once again.

This time I saw the ghost of Michael Morgan standing where, moments ago, there had been nothing! He was waving his arm beckoning for me to enter. The dim glow surrounding him provided just enough light for me to see inside the secret passageway, and what I saw were—spiders! A shiver ran through me. Goose bumps popped up at every pore. I saw the ghost calling and knew he was trying to guide me to the treasure. I wanted to wait for M.J. and Randi to return, but I was afraid the ghost might vanish again. I was afraid the treasure might not be found and that the poor ghost might be doomed to haunt the mansion forever.

I made a decision. Spiders or not, I had to follow the ghost. Leaving the secret door ajar as a clue to my whereabouts, I took a deep breath, gritted my teeth, and stepped into the spider-filled passage.

"I'm coming!" I called. "Lead me to the treasure. When I find it, you'll be free at last." The ghost nodded and began to float down the dark cobweb-filled passageway. Using his ghostly glow as my beacon, I followed, trying to block out the thought that creepy, crawly spiders were dangling all around me.

CHAPTER **Twelve**

"T HEY'RE only spiders," I mumbled to myself as I trailed after my ghostly guide. "Sp-spiders can't hurt me . . . I hope." I gulped and brushed aside a curtain of spider webs. It took every bit of courage I had to continue down that bleak, scary passageway. On and on the ghost led me as the narrow passageway twisted and turned beneath the old mansion.

"Ick! Yuck!" I grumbled as I cleared silky spider strands from my path. Every so often the ghost paused during our journey to look back and urge me on. I crept along like a snail for what seemed like hours. Finally, I turned a corner and came face to face with the biggest, ugliest spider web I had ever seen. It stretched from the bottom of the passageway to the top and from one side to the other. And clinging to the middle of the web was a big, hairy spider. On the other side of the web, the ghost floated, beckoning me to follow.

"I c-can't!" I sputtered shaking my head. "I can't go through that!" I was terrified of the large spider before me. My feet refused to take another step.

The ghost sensed my dilemma. He knew he had to help me overcome my fear if I was to help him. The ghost passed through the spider web like a breeze and came toward me. Then he reached out his hand, smiling in a way that seemed to say, "Don't be afraid." I reached out and took his hand. All of a sudden, I wasn't afraid. Led by the ghost, I used my free hand to swat the spider from its web and brush the tangled mess out of my way.

As soon as I was safely past the spider, the ghost released my hand. We turned another corner and entered a hidden room deep below the mansion. The ghost pointed at a large, oak chest in the middle of the room. It looked like the type used

long ago by pirates.

"It's the treasure," I whispered as I stared in awe at the old chest. The ghost nodded his head solemnly. I walked slowly forward. The chest was unlocked. I flipped open the lid. It was filled almost to the brim with shiny gold coins! It was a dazzling sight!

"It's the Morgan treasure!" I said to the ghost. "Now your family name will be restored to greatness!" I sniffed and wiped happy tears from my eyes. "Now you're free," I said. "You're free to rest."

Just then I heard someone shout my name. "Sandi! Where are you? Sandi? Answer me! Please!" It was my mom's voice. It was coming from the passageway. I also heard the clamor of footsteps. I looked back into the passageway and saw flashlight beams. I turned back toward my ghostly friend. The ghost smiled and then vanished without a trace.

"Mom! I'm here!" I yelled into the passageway. "I'm fine! Wait until you see what I found!"

"Sandi! Thank goodness you're okay," another

voice called. I recognized it as the voice of Miss Morgan.

"Sandi! Did you find it?" I heard Randi yell.

"Did you find the you-know-what?" M.J. called out. Apparently, an entire search party had come into the passageway to hunt for me.

"Yes!" I yelled back. "I found it! I found the treasure!"

Seconds later Mom, Miss Morgan, Randi, and M.J. emerged from the secret passageway and stepped into the hidden room.

"It's unbelievable!" Miss Morgan exclaimed when I showed her the chest full of coins. "This treasure must be worth a fortune! It's more than enough to refurbish the entire mansion and turn it into the Morgan Memorial Museum and Library."

"The ghost would like that," M.J. said. "He wants his family's name to be remembered forever."

"Ghost?" Mom muttered after she released me from her arms. Mom had spent the first few minutes of our reunion hugging the breath out of me. "What ghost?"

"Michael Morgan's ghost," Randi answered before I could speak. "He led Sandi to the treasure." Randi looked at me. "It was the ghost who led you to the treasure—wasn't it, Sandi?" she asked.

"It sure was," I said. "If it hadn't been for the ghost, I'd have never gotten past that last big spider web!"

"That's enough talk about ghosts," Mom ordered. "There are no such things as ghosts."

"Now you sound like Bobbi Joy, Mom," I said. "Ghosts really do exist."

"I think Sandy is right, Shelly," Miss Morgan said. She plucked a handful of gold coins from the pirate chest. "How much more proof do you need?"

Mom looked at Randi, then she looked at me. "You're right," she said. "I don't need any more proof. If Sandi and Randi say they saw a ghost— then I believe them!"

CHAPTER **Thirteen**

"I DON'T believe a word of this stupid ghost story," Bobbi Joy said stubbornly. "I think Sandi's story about how she found the treasure is a lot of baloney."

"Well, I saw the ghost, too, even if it was only one time," Randi argued.

"And what about Michael Morgan's diary?" M.J. added.

"I'm not falling for any more Daniels twins tricks," Bobbi Joy said. She folded her arms stubbornly across her chest.

"Quite frankly," said Mrs. Boikin, "I think Sandi stumbled upon the treasure chest by sheer luck."

Miss Morgan patted the lid of the treasure chest. "Luck or not," she said, as she opened the chest, "this treasure will make a lot of dreams come true. Not only is there enough money to repair the mansion, I'm sure there'll be enough left over for college funds for both M.J. and Annie." Miss Morgan looked at Randi and me. "And I think a reward is in order for the Daniels twins, too."

"My reward is knowing that the ghost of Michael Morgan is finally free," I said.

"Here we go with that ghost stuff again," Bobbi Joy complained.

"Da ghostie! Da ghostie!" Teddy yelled all of a sudden.

"Teddy," my mom said, "how many times do I have to tell you? You're not a ghostie!"

"He notta ghostie!" Annie corrected. "Da ghostie up dere!"

"Ghostie! Ghostie!" Teddy yelled again pointing at the staircase behind us.

We all did a slow turn to look where Teddy was

pointing. The staircase was glowing so brilliantly we had to shield our eyes with our hands. Hovering above the stairs was the ghost of Michael Morgan.

"It's the ghost!" I announced to everyone.

"I-I see him!" M.J. exclaimed happily. "I see him!"

"So do I!" Miss Morgan cried excitedly. "We all can see him!"

Mom shouted, "I can't believe it!"

The ghost of Michael Morgan looked down at me. I sensed I was seeing him for the last time. He smiled and I smiled back. He seemed so happy and peaceful.

"Good-bye, Sandi Daniels," the ghost said in a wavering voice. "Thank you!" There was a blinding flash of light. When I opened my eyes again, the ghost was gone.

"Dat ghostie wuz nice," Teddy said.

"He wuz bootiful!" Annie added.

"E-e-e-e-k!" Bobbi Joy screamed. "E-e-e-e-k! A real ghost!" Waving her arms wildly above her

head, she ran out of the foyer and into the library shrieking at the top of her lungs.

"Bobbi Joy! Come back!" Mrs. Boikin pleaded as she raced after her terrified daughter. "Calm down! Mommy won't let that big bad ghost harm you!"

"I notta fraid of dat ghostie," Teddy said.

"Neither was I," Randi said as she winked at Teddy and Annie.

"Wish we could say the same for Bobbi Joy," M.J. said, teasing. "She vanished faster than the ghost did!" We all laughed.

"I a pie-rat now!" Teddy yelled as he began to race around the treasure chest.

"I get you!" Annie hollered as she started after my little brother.

"I'll get both of you!" I shouted. I raised my arms in the air like a ghost. "Now I da ghostie!"

ABOUT THE Author

MICHAEL J. PELLOWSKI was born January 24, 1949, in New Brunswick, New Jersey. He is a graduate of Rutgers, the State University of New Jersey, and has a degree in education. Before turning to writing, Michael was a professional football player and then a high school teacher.

Michael has written more than 125 books for children. When he's not writing books, Michael enjoys fishing with his family, as well as jogging and exercising.